"Was that—is the driver firing at us?"

"The passenger is. We need to get out of here." Heath lifted her upright then pulled her toward the tree line as the approaching car's engine roared closer. "Can you run?"

"I...yes." She was breathless, her head spinning. Her burner phone was still in the car. "The phone is still in the—"

"Move." Heath pressed his palm to her lower back to guide her deeper into the forest. "If something happens, keep running. Find a spot to hide."

"Wait...my cell—"

"There's no time. There are two men in that car." He pushed her forward, and her brain erupted with a volcano of questions and fear. Did he think he would get shot?

The vehicle's engine noise increased, then cut off. Silence followed, except for their frantic footsteps among the pine needles and ferns. One *slam* sounded, echoing into the woods after her and Heath like a warning. The second *slam* sent liquid fire through her veins.

"They're in the woods too. Keep going!"

Kerry Johnson is an award-winning author who has been conversing with fictional characters and devouring books since her childhood in the Connecticut woods. A longtime member of American Christian Fiction Writers, she lives on the sunny, stormy west coast of Florida with her husband, two sons, her niece and way too many books. She loves Jesus, long walks, all creatures great and small, and a hot cup of tea all hours of the day.

Books by Kerry Johnson

Love Inspired Suspense

Snowstorm Sabotage
Tunnel Creek Ambush
Christmas Forest Ambush
Hidden Mountain Secrets
Hunted in the Forest
Abducted in the Woods
Targeted in the Swamp

Visit the Author Profile page at LoveInspired.com.

TARGETED IN THE SWAMP

KERRY JOHNSON

LOVE INSPIRED SUSPENSE
INSPIRATIONAL ROMANCE

MIX
Paper | Supporting responsible forestry
FSC® C021394
FSC www.fsc.org

LOVE INSPIRED® SUSPENSE
INSPIRATIONAL ROMANCE

PLEASE RECYCLE THIS PRODUCT IS RECYCLABLE
Recycling programs for this product may not exist in your area.

ISBN-13: 978-1-335-95767-2

Targeted in the Swamp

For questions and comments about the quality of this book, please contact us at CustomerService@Harlequin.com.

Love Inspired
22 Adelaide St. West, 41st Floor
Toronto, Ontario M5H 4E3, Canada
www.LoveInspired.com

HarperCollins Publishers
Macken House, 39/40 Mayor Street Upper,
Dublin 1, D01 C9W8, Ireland
www.HarperCollins.com

Printed in Lithuania

And he said unto me, My grace is sufficient for thee:
for my strength is made perfect in weakness.
—*2 Corinthians* 12:9

Jesus, thank You for being my strength when I am weak and the brightest Light unto my path.

ONE

Laurel Bell slowed as she approached Black Ash Swamp, then tugged the area map from her pack. She eyed the topographical lines and squiggles of Allegheny National Forest on paper. Her Nikon Z9 hung around her neck, a familiar friend and comforting weight as she began a new chapter in her life.

She frowned at the map then took in her surroundings. Black-trunked trees and slime-coated rocks edged the swamp's shallow, scummy water, highlighted by late-spring sunshine. A rotted, partially submerged log platformed two turtles, but they dived beneath the water when she tucked the map in her pack. Almost immediately their heads broke the surface again.

"I'm still here." Laurel grinned at the turtles' antics, but her smile slipped as she looked around. Molly Calhoun, the other forest ranger who was supposed to meet her, wasn't here yet.

She found the end of her long braid and rubbed her fingertips across the wispy hair. The US Forest Service had hired her on as a wildlife photography ranger serving the Holloway District, and assistant head ranger Tucker Brindley had asked her to photograph a recently discovered primitive campsite in the swamp. Molly—a friendly botanist and longtime resident of Holloway—offered to meet her here because she had to check on an invasive plant species' growth. A nature and wildlife photographer, Laurel was the only person on staff in the Holloway District qualified and available to document the campsite discovery, and Tucker had seemed grateful she was available to send out.

An osprey shrieked overhead. She recoiled at the startling cry, then uncapped her Nikon. The majestic bird soared through the sky, gliding on the wind. She snapped a couple of shots, zoomed in for two more, then aimed the viewfinder at the landscape. Several clicks calmed her and satisfied the urge to document the lush green foliage. Normally, being out in the woods alone wasn't a problem. In fact, it was what she enjoyed most about her work. The peacefulness and solitude. But today was the anniversary of her dad's murder, and no amount of sunshine would lift her spirits. Laurel traced a fingertip around the Nikon's lens. After twenty years in the WITSEC program, she still battled for control over her emotions and the lurking memories.

She'd been nine when her dad was murdered while they biked on one of Redwood National Park's trails. Even with twenty-five hundred miles separating her from the place where Dad was killed and her life drastically changed, that one event always proved impossible to hide from. Sorrow followed her across the country and shadowed each year of her life.

Two decades ago, her dad, a veteran detective with the San Francisco PD, had busted a group of criminals colluding in illegal activity in the back of a laundromat on a quiet corner in the Bayview District. He had pulled out his weapon upon entering the back room and found millions in drug money along with a pile of weapons on a table. Six surprised men faced him, armed to the teeth. He wounded three of them and killed the other three before he was shot in the side and the leg just as his backup arrived.

She curled forward. If only he'd never investigated that tip about the laundromat that morning, he might still be here with her.

If only the consequences of that day hadn't followed him to the Redwood Trail.

If only.

She straightened, angling her face toward the bright blue sky. It was beautiful out here, a different kind of beauty than Northern California. Less rugged. Peaceful, less busy, with winding roads crossing emerald forests. She'd only been in northwest Pennsylvania for a week, but already she felt at home.

You can do this, Laurel.

"Lauralee." She tested her old name out, the one her mom and dad had given her, but it sounded strange. Foreign. Then she shook her head and adjusted her pack, resuming her trek around the swamp. The primitive campsite sat a quarter mile past the main portion of the swamp, under a grove of northern white cedar at the end of the hiking trail encircling the connected bodies of water. She might as well find the site and prep the scene for pictures.

The unmistakable crunch of twigs in the woods she'd just walked through froze her midstride.

She turned, her gaze swinging across the isolated landscape. "Molly?"

No answer, only the osprey's intermittent screaming overhead. The sharp sound sent a wave of goose bumps over her skin. Several more steps commenced, quieter yet growing closer. Slow footsteps that made her pulse drum in her temples. A stunning sense of déjà vu clung to her like a spiderweb.

She shot another wild look around. Thick stands of Black Ash trees stood between her and the parking lot, where her trusty Subaru Forester was parked. To her back, swamps and hundreds of acres of forest.

As with much of her life, she was utterly alone.

A man broke through the foliage, dark clothes covering his muscular frame and a black ski mask hiding his face. His strides were rapid and sure, and even from thirty or forty yards away his eyes were frighteningly intent. Instantly Laurel knew she was his target.

She snatched her radio from her belt and mashed the talk button while backtracking. "This is Ranger Campbell—I mean, Bell." *Campbell.* Laurel was thrown back twenty years, when she had to use her dad's flip phone to call for help after he'd been shot. She'd given her real name then, Lauralee Campbell. "It's Ranger Bell. I'm at Black Ash Swamp. There's a m-man following me, not a hiker. He's wearing a mask. P-please help."

A scream erupted from her throat when her pursuer launched into a loping run, a hungry coyote after its prey. Laurel turned and tore away from him, clutching the radio like it was a weapon. Her camera smacked against her middle and her backpack constricted her stride as she ran. She whipped her pack off and flung it, then did the same with her camera. Finally unencumbered, she kicked into a sprint again. She needed to get turned around to make it to her car. The key fob for her Forester jangled in her pocket as she beelined for the main trail. It wound around the back of the swamp, ending up in the parking lot. If she could outrace him, keep him far enough away, she could get into her car and get to safety. Call the police.

Had anyone received her radio message?

The wind wailed as she leaped over the muddy ground. *Who was this?* The last check-in she'd had with Tim Polling, her WITSEC handler, had confirmed that her dad's killer had recently been denied parole. This couldn't be him—the man she had shot and wounded after he had murdered her dad and then testified against at the tender age of ten.

August Basile is locked up for life, Tim had told her.

August Basile, son of notorious San Francisco gangster Leonard Basile, couldn't touch her now. Tim promised her that, a small buoy of reassurance amid the tumultuous waves of her life.

Who was this stranger coming after her then? A sob built in her chest.

"Please help!" *Please, God.*

Despite her terror, praying still felt hopeless. Futile. After all, God had let her dad die. He took her mom away when she was so young. All the childhood pain, all the hurt prickled across her skin as she ran for her life.

She launched over a rotted stump on the other side of the swamp, but misjudged the width. Her foot caught on the slippery edge, and she crashed through a low wall of buttonbush, knocking into rocks and sticks that jabbed her shins through the ranger uniform. Her legs wobbled when she rose, then she stumbled forward, almost face-planting again.

Her pursuer's winded panting and steady footsteps closed in.

Laurel hooked a sharp left once she came upon the trail that circled the interconnected swamps, her muscles on fire.

A hand seized her ranger shirt, and a powerful force jerked her back. She screamed. The man's iron grip made her feel like a doll tossed from a child's bed. She cried out as the momentum caused them to crash together to the ground. Laurel rolled over slimy stones, twigs, and clumps of mud then ended up splashing into a shallow body of water. She crawled away on all fours, panting, but when she tried to stand her pursuer snatched her ankles and pulled her back in.

Clumps of swamp milkweed clung to her cheeks and face as she fought to get away. Her attacker's hands were tentacles, wrapping around her shoulders and hauling her into deeper water. She struggled, kicking out. Cinching her hips upward to lash at him with her legs.

"Let me go!"

He remained eerily quiet, his dark brown eyes pinned on hers as he resisted her fighting posture. August Basile's eyes had been crystal-clear blue, flat and hard when he murdered her dad. This monster's gaze was filled with a cold determination that turned her heart to ice. The murky water slurped under his boots as he toyed with her like an alligator with its kill.

"It's almost over," he mocked her.

"No!" She kicked out again, trying to get away. *He's going to drown me. Please, God. Help.* Would God hear her after all these years of silence?

Be brave, baby girl, her dad had rasped out as his hand found hers, protecting her just moments after he was shot. Ten seconds later his last rattling breath announced he'd left earth and joined her mom in Heaven.

Now her attacker loomed above her in the water, hands clutching her upper arms like a hawk with a rabbit in its talons. Then he plunged her under.

Laurel slammed her mouth shut and tried to open her eyes, but they stung and she couldn't focus. She kept fighting, digging her nails into his skin. The seconds ticked off mercilessly, each one depleting her air. Finally, when her heart felt like it would burst, he lifted her above the surface. She gasped, sucking in oxygen before he chuckled and dipped her below the surface again.

Each time under seemed longer, until her legs weighed

twice as much, and her lungs burned. Her arms were useless strings attached to her body.

When he lifted her from the water and tossed her several feet, into the sludge at the edge of the swamp, pain coiled across her rib cage. She gasped for oxygen and tried to move, tried to crawl away, but her muscles weren't responding. The whole world spun. Then he grabbed her feet and drew her back into the water.

He's playing with me. Toying with me before he kills me.

Laurel fought her attacker as he submerged her again. Kicked. Wriggled. Punched at his midsection. But he was out of reach, and she was no match for his greater weight and strength.

Please, God, she prayed again as the world turned hazy and an image of her dad filled her clouded mind. *Daddy, I tried to be brave.*

Heath Calhoun touched the green button on his cell. His sister Molly's smiling face filled the screen, then he returned his eyes to the road. "What's up, sis?"

"Where are you?" Molly sounded breathless. Upset.

He straightened from a slouch in the truck's driver-side bucket seat. He'd dropped off his daughter, Piper, in Hershey, where his in-laws lived, for a couple days. Now he headed back into Holloway to start on overdue house repair projects during his couple of days off work at the Police Department. "Dropped Piper off, now I'm heading home. What's up?"

"I just got to Black Ash Swamp. I'm meeting a new ranger, Laurel. But when I parked and got out, I heard screaming. And her car's here but I don't see her."

He noted his location. Three-point-five miles past Black Ash. Heath checked for oncoming traffic, then decelerated and swung through the other lane in a wide U-turn. He straightened the truck then pressed the gas, heading back toward the remote, wetlands area of Allegheny National Forest.

"Is there anyone else there today?" he asked his younger sister.

"No. No hikers. Only her car."

"You're sure that's hers?"

"Yes. When I met Laurel the other day, she was at the ranger station with Tucker. I saw her get out of a little dark green Subaru SUV with West Virginia plates."

"I'm on my way. ETA three minutes." He leaned sideways and opened the glove compartment, grabbing his Glock. "Stay in your truck. Lock the doors. I'll call Tucker."

"Okay. Thank you for coming out, Heath."

"Be there ASAP. I mean it—stay put!"

Heath placed the weapon on the console then accelerated until the engine revved. Molly had been through enough when she and her fiancé, FBI special cyberagent Eli Buchanan, had become pawns in a cat-and-mouse game with a wanted cybercriminal last year. Molly was days away from marrying Eli, and despite Heath's initial dislike of Eli because he broke Molly's heart when they were eighteen, Heath had come to value her fiancé's place in their lives. Heath was pleased to see his loving sister finally being taken care of and cherished like she deserved.

He eyed his speedometer as he neared the turn for the swamp. Fifteen over with one mile to go. He should've installed flashing lights on his truck.

At least Piper wasn't with him. That would've made this much more complicated. And his poor daughter's life—minus her mom—had been rough enough.

Heath called Tucker and checked in, quickly briefing him on the situation. Tucker shared about Laurel's cry for help over the radio and mentioned that another new hire, forestry firefighter Clay Reiger, was in the area and would meet Heath there within ten minutes.

Heath hung up when the wooden sign for Black Ash Swamp appeared. He slowed then took a sharp right. The sloped gravel road to the swamp parking lot was about three-quarters of a mile, and he doubled the twenty-five-mile-per-hour speed limit as his gaze roved the area. He made out a white US Forest Service truck beside a hunter green Forester. As Molly noted, no sign of another vehicle, but there was a second lot about one-third of a mile north, plus various campsites farther down the main road with paths that connected to the swamp.

First things first, he had to make sure his sister and the new ranger were safe.

His cell rang, and he grabbed it. "Calhoun here."

"Sergeant Calhoun, this is ranger Clay Reiger. I'm nearby. ETA eight minutes."

"Hey, Clay. I appreciate the backup in case there's an injury." Heath had met Clay twice now, and learned the former Air Force firefighter reservist who specialized in forest fire management seemed like a smart, responsible guy. "I'm on my way in now."

They ended the call, and he parked, grabbed his weapon, slipped his cell in his back pocket then dashed over to Molly's truck. Heath narrowed his eyes as he confirmed his sister wasn't in the vehicle. He turned and jogged down the trail. Sure, Molly had taken self-defense classes at Eli's request—another thing that had endeared Eli to Heath—but she was no match for an armed attacker.

He eyed the trampled ground as he rushed up the trail. His sister's heart was too big for her head. Or was it that she led with her heart over her head? Whatever. The bottom line was Molly forgot to exercise caution when it came to her safety.

"Molly?" he called out.

"Heath!" His sister's panicked voice carried over from the largest body of water. "She's back here, and she's hurt!"

"On my way." Lord willing, this new ranger wasn't wounded badly. A twisted ankle, perhaps, from the muddy ground. Or a snake bite. His Epi-pen kit sat in the back seat. He should've brought that along. What was her name? *Laurel.* Tucker had shared about the new US Forest Service hire during their call, and Molly had also mentioned Laurel yesterday in passing when she'd stopped over from their dad's place to drop off an extra casserole. His sister enjoyed trying new recipes, and he and Piper were the grateful recipients.

He kicked up his pace as he entered the trail encircling the pond, then slowed and took a left where it connected to a bike path that stretched ten miles deeper into Allegheny National Forest. Ferns clung to the pathway, swishing against his jeans, and his skin dampened with sweat-fueled adrenaline.

He slowed, scanning the tree line. "Where are you?"

"Here. Hurry!" Molly's answer didn't lend him any peace of mind.

Molly's tan-and-red hiking boots caught his eye through the thickets. He bisected the foliage, slowing as the earth softened, slurping at his shoes when he neared the sodden back edge of the swamp.

"Moll, what happened—"

His jaw unhinged. A petite woman lay in the muck beside his crouching sister. Tangled, damp hair the color of his morning coffee fanned out from a pale face. The victim appeared unconscious. *Lord, have mercy.*

"Is she breathing?" Heath sank to his knees, pressing two fingers to her carotid artery. He sagged in relief at the steady *thump, thump* of life beneath her splotchy skin. "Did you see anyone when you got here?" he asked Molly.

"No, just her. I heard her screams, then I called you."

Heath whipped out his cell and hit 9-1-1, then handed Molly the phone. He checked the other ranger's face for wounds and lightly touched the damp, red marks marring her cheeks. "Tell them what you found and where we are. I'm going to—"

Molly screamed and scrambled sideways. Heath leaped to his feet and turned as a masked man exploded from the forest behind them, dressed in dark camo, a formidable knife in his grasp.

"Law enforcement! Drop the knife or I will shoot." Heath feinted right and drew his gun, but the attacker rushed him again before the safety was off and the weapon was aimed. Heath sprang away, his grip on his gun precariously slippery from the water on the victim's face.

His gut told him there'd be no de-escalating this situation. He was forced to either attempt to fire and miss while taking a knife to his torso or lose the shot but avoid being stabbed. He chose the latter, and as he faked and turned, he came around behind the attacker and drove one knee into his lower back. Something hot prickled his side, and he jerked away mid-shove. The man landed on the ground with a resounding *thud*, but then he jumped up and bounded out of reach.

Heath's shoes splashed in the swamp as he backed up, Molly's warning cry echoing in his eardrums. He flicked off the safety and steadied his aim as the man advanced once more, his gaze darting between Heath and the woman on the ground.

Sweat stung his eyes as images of Duke Ridley's lifeless body flashed through his mind.

God, help me.

The attacker growled out a curse then spun and took off, busting through the foliage the same way Heath had minutes ago. The forest swallowed him whole. Heath's muscles shivered from the altercation, and the urge to give chase gripped his limbs. But he couldn't leave his sister and the wounded ranger. There'd be time to find the offender later.

Heath glanced down to see his light blue T-shirt turning black on his side. *Just great.* He'd been stabbed on his day off.

TWO

Laurel flinched awake from a series of male grunts that sounded terribly close. Then the loud thud of two bodies hitting the ground followed. A shout, then a feminine shriek. She tried to move, to raise her head, but her muscles wouldn't cooperate. A curse tainted the air, then fleeing footsteps pounded the ground. Laurel blinked frantically to clear her vision.

"He's gone," a man huffed. "Backup will be here any minute."

"Heath, you're bleeding," a woman replied.

"It's a little cut. I'm fine." The man, Heath's, voice was deep and soft, so much like her dad's that she turned toward it. She attempted to push air up her throat to speak, to tell them she was awake, but it burned badly and the words never came. Suddenly water shot up from her lungs, into the back of her mouth, and she turned to her side, sputtering, gagging and spitting out the grimy water. She felt like a newborn babe, helpless and unable to communicate.

The woman kneeled beside her, setting a gentle hand on Laurel's shoulder. A hazy memory floated through her mind, all the way back from childhood. Before Mom was taken from them in a car accident. Laurel struggling to sleep, worrying about her dad and his job, and her mom padding into her bedroom at midnight to rub her back and help calm her fears.

Laurel had often fallen asleep with her mom's hands on her, and this woman's tender touch was like mom's. Soft, sure.

"Laurel, it's me. Molly Calhoun? From the ranger station? I'm so sorry I was late."

Laurel drew in a sputtery breath. But another liquid cough caught in her lungs, and acrid swamp water filled her mouth. She turned sideways and released the nasty water from her system, shivering and curling in a ball when she was done. Heat climbed the tender skin of her neck that these two strangers were witnessing her throwing up and in this incapacitated state.

The man's voice startled her again, and she shifted her head and blinked hard. He was standing over her, a cell to his ear.

Almost like he was standing guard.

"I need two officers out at the swamp. Right. I'll leave markers. Yes, a masked man…not certain if he's armed other than a large hunting knife. Attempted murder. No, the new ranger at the swamp. That's correct. She seems stable. Right, he did come after me. I was unable to de-escalate, and he took off. No shots fired. The attacker? Headed southeast. Molly and I are good. Right. No, I'm not sure if he has a gun. That works."

"Heath, you're not *good*," Molly snapped. "You were stabbed."

"It's a cut, Moll."

"Is he…gone?" Laurel found her voice, though it was barely a strained whisper.

"He's gone." Molly's shaky tone contradicted her answer. The woman reached down, swiping carefully at Laurel's jawline. Was she wiping…tears? Laurel hadn't realized she'd begun crying. Or maybe she'd been crying the whole time.

Reality was a bolt of lightning on a cloudless day.

Someone had tried—almost successfully—to kill her. *Attempted murder.* She couldn't comprehend it, couldn't believe after all these years of hiding that someone had come after her. The thin mirage of safety she'd wrapped herself in since Dad's death cracked like a windowpane beneath a baseball. Her muscles quivered, shaking so hard she couldn't control them, and her teeth chattered as though she'd been locked in a freezer for an hour.

The man crouched, scrutinizing Laurel briefly as he joined Molly. This must be Heath.

"Can you wiggle your fingers and toes for me, ma'am?"

She frowned, desperate to do what he asked. Her nails slid into the muddy ground, and her toes bumped into her hiking shoes, damp inside her socks.

"I can."

"Good. Appears there's no spinal injury." He paused, his attention shifting to their surroundings again. "She's going into shock. I've got an emergency blanket in my truck. Let's get her there and keep her warm."

"Shouldn't we wait for the ambulance?"

"It'll take them too long to get out here. I don't want to stay here with the attacker on the loose any longer than necessary."

He swept his arms under Laurel, lifting her easily. Every inch of her body cried out despite his careful motions, and when she winced and met his hazel eyes, concern and determination shone in their depths.

Laurel tried to speak, but the whole-body shaking kept her tongue from working right. Her jaw felt stiff, and suddenly she was bitterly cold despite the sunshine. So cold.

Heath motioned Molly ahead of him and followed at a fast walk.

"I need to be able to see you," he barked, then looked down at Laurel. "I've got you now."

Damp wisps of her hair blew across her face as he increased his pace. The braid she'd hurriedly twined together earlier today must've come loose when she'd been submerged. Laurel shivered, and his strides increased in intensity as though he understood her fear. For a few blessed moments she felt safe in this stranger's arms.

Was this what it was like to be held, to be protected? She'd never allowed anyone close to her. Never gotten caught up in a relationship like so many high school and college friends and acquaintances. Because of WITSEC, she'd stayed on the outskirts of social circles, friendly enough to just fit in but guarding her heart and time. Watching what she said. Who she was around. What social situations she committed to.

Because she couldn't stand the thought of losing anyone else.

The *slap*, *slap* of his shoes on pavement told her they'd made it to the parking lot. They jogged up to a large four-door truck.

"You're going to ride with me. Can you sit up, or would you rather lay in the back seat?" Heath asked.

"I can…sit." Her tongue stuck to the roof of her mouth as he moved around the truck, opened the door and gently placed her in the front passenger seat. Then he pulled a bag from the back seat, unzipped it and placed a large, dark green blanket over her legs and torso. Molly popped up beside him and leaned across Heath to help buckle Laurel's seat belt.

"Here." Heath handed Laurel an unopened water bottle. "No doubt you swallowed swamp water. I recommend rinsing your mouth out."

Laurel accepted the bottle then uncapped it and tipped it up, emptying enough to fill her cheeks and mouth. Heath stepped back as she swished the water then leaned out the open truck door and spat. Then she did it again, watching dazedly at the darkening puddle on the concrete beside the truck.

"Better?" he asked as she handed him the half-empty bottle.

She wiped her mouth and nodded.

Molly whispered something, then Heath whistled.

"I have some bad news," he motioned behind him. "It appears your attacker broke into your car, probably before he came after you." Laurel straightened in the truck and squinted at her driver-side window. She gasped at the gaping hole and fractured glass haloing it. "Did you have valuables inside?"

Oh no. "My purse and wallet. But my cell is in my pack..."

"Where's that?" he asked.

"When the man came after me, I tossed it. My camera, too."

Heath trotted over to her Forester and briefly inspected the car without touching anything. When he returned, he shook his head. "I don't see a purse inside. The guy must've nabbed it." He addressed Molly. "Let's go."

"I'll follow you there." Molly backtracked toward her white truck.

"I'd like you to ride with me."

"What— I can't leave my truck. I'll just drive behind you into town."

"I need you to ride with me," Heath repeated, his voice pitched lower, almost a command.

Laurel swiveled her head to catch Molly and Heath holding a silent conversation, their facial expressions and an occasional flung arm punctuating more clearly than words would.

Evidently, they were quite familiar with each other. Were they a couple? Laurel had offered to shoot Molly and her fiancé's upcoming wedding pictures after their photographer cancelled due to unforeseen circumstances. She couldn't remember Molly's fiancé's name.

Heath sent Molly a final stern look, which she returned with a withering scowl. "It's safest for all of us if you ride with me to the hospital."

"You are being impossible."

"Only because I care." He held his palms out in a placating gesture.

Laurel blanched. She hated hospitals. Hated their smell and the sounds. Hated the way they reminded her of the day her dad died, when she'd sat there for hours until a nurse contacted her dad's supervisor at SFPD. After that she'd been taken by a patient police officer to meet the Heigels for the first time.

Her eyes prickled, and she snuggled deeper into the blanket. Right now, the urge to disappear, to turn invisible, overwhelmed her. It was one of the aspects of entering Witness Protection that she'd mastered well—blending in. Remaining unnoticed.

But it hadn't helped today. Someone had found her.

Molly bounced into the back seat as Heath loaded in on the driver's side. The large vehicle had a compact computer on the console, and a hand-held radio sat on the dash.

Just then a US Forest Service truck pulled into the parking lot beside them. A lean, dark-haired man jumped out and treaded over to Heath's window.

"Reiger," Heath greeted him.

"Sergeant Calhoun." The other man wore a forest service uniform, and a scar puckered his right forearm, peeking out near the neckline of his ranger shirt. She tried not to stare.

This must be Clay Reiger, the other new hire. She hadn't met him yet, and when his gaze met hers, his light eyes widened.

"Is she okay?"

"Mild throat lacerations. Bumps and bruises. Inhaled some swamp water. Nothing appears broken, thankfully. We're headed to the hospital now." Heath described where Laurel had been attacked then checked his cell. "Her pack and camera are out there still. I would recommend waiting for the HPD backup before entering the swamp. ETA is four minutes. The attacker is masked, has a knife, and is a definite threat. I don't know if he's armed otherwise."

"Will do."

They said goodbye, then Heath pulled out of the parking lot. Periodically he checked the rearview mirror. When his phone rang, he tossed it to Molly.

"It's Tucker. Update him, please."

"She's with us." Molly briefly explained Laurel's condition. "We're on our way to Holloway General."

They finished up, then she handed the phone back to Heath. "He said to keep him posted. He's on his way to the swamp now."

"I hope they catch him." Heath's hands had a death grip on the steering wheel when he addressed Laurel. "Molly said you're a new ranger here in Holloway, and you do photography?"

"Yes," she responded, her voice still raspy.

"Were you by chance able to get any pictures of the man who attacked you?"

Laurel closed her eyes. "I don't think so, but I can check when I get my camera back." She reopened them. "I took a couple shots of an osprey overhead just before he came out of the woods." She shivered.

"The photographer we hired to take pictures at our wedding had a family situation arise and had to cancel," Molly interjected. "Laurel agreed to fill in this weekend." She hesitated. "But only if you're feeling well enough. I totally understand if—"

"I can still do it." Laurel licked her swollen lips. Molly said *our* wedding. So, she and Heath were engaged. She clasped the water bottle he'd offered her earlier and gulped down another sip of water, the liquid catching in her throat. She coughed several times, and Heath glanced her way in concern.

"I imagine your throat is going to be sore for a couple days."

She placed the water bottle back in the cup holder, her grip shaky.

"So, what were you taking pictures of at Black Ash Swamp?" he asked.

"Hikers found shards of old pottery in the woods behind the swamp last week." Molly jumped in. "Looks like a primitive campsite. Tucker feels terrible that he sent her out there."

"It's not his fault." Laurel ran her fingertips along the tender skin of her neck.

"If *I'd* been there on time, maybe this wouldn't have happened." Molly patted Laurel's arm. So far, she had proved to be a kind and supportive person and coworker, and Laurel was grateful to have her on her side.

"*You've* been through enough," Heath admonished Molly. "Thank the Lord you're both okay."

Heath was a believer. Maybe Molly, too? The realization calmed Laurel's heart as she gazed out at the forest. While her faith had been deflated by life's difficulties, she appreciated knowing she was in the care of those who trusted in God, even though she struggled to do just that.

"Whereabouts you from?" He flung one wrist over the

steering wheel and set his other arm across the driver-side door handle, tapping his fingers against it.

"West Virginia." Her WITSEC handler, Tim, had stressed how vital it was that she get in touch with him first before sharing any details about being in Witness Protection, even with law enforcement. All her life she'd learned to be honest but vague in her answers, and since she couldn't tell Heath that she was in Witness Protection, she'd have to be cautious with her answers until she spoke with Tim.

"Is that right." He sent her a brief but searing assessment that made her squirm. "I don't think I officially introduced myself. I'm Sergeant Heath Calhoun with Holloway PD. Also Molly's overprotective older brother."

Her mouth dropped open. He was Molly's brother. *Not* her fiancé. Why this news sent relief through her limbs, she wasn't sure. No wonder he'd been so demanding back there.

What would that be like, to have a sister or brother to look out for her? To call just to check in? Her parents had never been able to have more children. Her mom was forty-two when she had Laurel, her dad forty-five. She was their miracle baby, though Laurel wished God would've held off on the miracles and saved her mom's life that foggy morning on the road and her dad's life on that trail instead.

"Heath can be a pain, but he means well," Molly teased.

"Someone has to look out for you."

Molly playfully flicked his broad shoulder. "Yeah, yeah."

A wistful smile worked over Laurel's face. "I'm just grateful you were both there today."

"Me, too. You'll feel better once you're checked out at the hospital," Molly tried to assure her.

Laurel tucked the top edge of the blanket around her shoulders and closed her eyes. A cold chill climbed her spine.

The tremulous sense of safety she'd felt after moving here

had disappeared the moment she'd spotted her attacker at the swamp. August Basile might be behind bars, but someone else was after her. The man had tried to kill her and likely wouldn't give up now. She wasn't sure that she'd ever feel *better* again.

Heath pulled into the emergency room parking entrance, his mind spinning faster than bald tires on black ice. Who would go after a forest ranger like this—and why?

He exited his truck and came around to the passenger-side door to help Laurel out. After removing the blanket and unbuckling her seat belt, he offered his hand. She stared at it with a brief look of panic, which quickly subsided, but it confirmed his first instinct. *Someone* had manhandled this lovely young woman. Scared the living daylights out of her.

Not just today, but before. In her past.

Anger flushed up his neck. As an officer of the law, he'd taken an oath to protect and defend the population from those who would seek to steal, harm and destroy others. But woman-beaters? Those men he had to watch himself with, because as a brother of three sisters, a father, a son and a husband, he would never stand by and allow those he loved to come to harm by a criminal.

Heath shook off the suppressed fury and offered his arm. When she lightly slipped hers beneath his, his chest lifted at the tiny victory of trust. Even with the dirt smudging her face, sludge-caked hair and saturated clothing, she was an attractive woman, one who needed protection.

Stop it, Calhoun.

His thoughts alarmed him. For so long he'd only had eyes for his wife. Kara's unexpected death from a rare heart condition they'd discovered—too late—had broken something inside him. After he and Piper lost her, the thought of dating anyone else had been the furthest thing from his mind. He was a single father now, not a bachelor on the prowl. Piper needed him, and whatever energy was left over from that he focused on the rest of his family and then work.

Molly climbed out and faced them, surveying Laurel's clothes before addressing him. "I can run over to your house and grab some of my extra clothes for her to change into. Would that be okay, Laurel?"

"Yes, please, that would be great. Thank you." Laurel's whispered words were hard to hear, but her sincerity rang loud and clear.

"I should be back in half an hour." His sister eyed him with a speculative expression he recognized immediately.

He scowled. *She's wounded. I'm being gentlemanly and helpful. That's it.*

She's very pretty. Molly's expressive brows and bright eyes did all the talking.

He narrowed his to slits.

"Be careful." He handed off the truck key fob and turned, steering Laurel toward the emergency room entrance and in the process escaping his sister's presumptuous stare. Once they stepped through the huge sliding doors, pops of sterile white filled his peripheral vision, and the scent of antiseptic cleaners assailed his senses. Laurel seemed to shrink on his arm the deeper into the hospital they treaded.

After losing Kara in this very hospital, he got it.

"Sergeant Calhoun, what can I do for you today?"

Tinsley Spiller's exaggerated Southern drawl carried across the lobby, and he carefully rotated Laurel and himself so he could meet her eyes. The bottle blonde had been more than obvious about her interest in him since a few months after Kara's death. She was too young, too friendly, too… everything. His wife's endearing beauty was an inside-out package that had been a rare treasure, and he knew he'd never find that again, especially not with Tinsley Spiller.

"Tinsley, how's it going? This is Laurel. She's a new ranger with the US Forest Service." He lowered his voice. "We just came from Black Ash Swamp. Laurel was the victim of an assault and needs to see a doctor ASAP."

"Oh, gracious. That is so scary. Any idea who went after her?"

"No, ma'am, and you know I can't comment on that." He cleared his throat as Tinsley scrutinized Laurel, her megawatt smile dimming. "We just need to get her through inpatient quickly. Please."

"Does she have her license and insurance card?"

"No, they were stolen from her car."

"Goodness gracious. Okay. I'll go grab the shift nurse. In the meantime, she'll need to fill out a few admittance forms."

Laurel accepted the medical tablet with trembling hands. Tinsley pointed to the waiting room. "That's for noninfectious patients."

It sat empty, and Laurel's form slumped as though relieved. They made their way over to it, and Laurel carefully disengaged from Heath and hobbled to a chair, practically falling into it. A moment later, she looked up, her smooth forehead creased.

"You need to be seen, too. You're bleeding."

"It's just a poke." He sank into the chair two over from hers to give her space. "I've had my tetanus booster. I'll get checked out once I know you're okay."

She tapped away at the screen for a couple of minutes, and Heath leaned the back of his head on the wall, scrubbing a palm down his face. "You ever been in the ER before?"

"Yes." A faraway expression settled over her pale features.

"Sprained wrist. My dad and I were biking the Golden Gate Trail…" She paused, mouth slack, suddenly stricken.

He straightened. "What's wrong?"

"I'm just sore and my throat hurts. My stomach is kind of upset, too." She laid the tablet on her legs then rubbed her closed eyelids. When she reopened them and looked his way, he noted the darker circle of blue around the light brown pupil. Unusual.

"Unfortunately, there's no RO filter on the swamp water." His jaw tightened as he examined her. "He got you pretty good here." Heath reached out, grazing her red-rimmed skin beneath her chin with his fingertips, then yanked his arm back.

He didn't know this young woman, and it didn't take a detective to recognize that she wouldn't welcome being touched, even if he was trying to help her. Twenty minutes later, when he led her into the hospital room, she held herself stiff against him. Away from him.

When she started speaking to the ER doctor, his thoughts mushroomed.

Had the man who attacked her been an abusive ex-boyfriend? Or ex-husband? Broken marriages coupled with spousal abuse were especially difficult cases after being raised by his parents, a pastor father and a loving mom who had an ideal marriage. As a police officer, he'd seen too many tragic situations with abuse, and it never got easier. Every day he prayed God would keep his heart from hardening toward his fellow man. But when a man treated a woman this way…

His muscles turned to ice.

You have to watch the thoughts you think, Daddy. Piper's Dr. Seuss version of Philippians 4:8 reminded him about this very problem. "Finally, brethren, whatsoever things are true, whatsoever things are honest, whatsoever things are just, whatsoever things are pure, whatsoever things are lovely, whatsoever things are of good report; if there be any virtue, and if there be any praise, think on these things."

Add to that what happened at the Danson's home, which was seared into Heath's memory. Duke Ridley, a welder at Holloway Sheet Metal, had been kicked out by his wife because his alcoholism had splintered their marriage. Days later Duke broke into Carl Danson's house to get to the elder man's stocked liquor cabinet and ended up finding Carl's shotgun collection as well. When Heath and his back-up arrived, Duke was stone cold drunk, waving one of the gleaming shotguns around. He'd refused to drop the weapon after multiple warnings, instead pretending to aim it at Heath and the other deputy. Heath had no other choice but to take Duke out.

He would never forget the stark look of shock and hurt on the poor man's face before he fell to the floor.

Heath still saw it in his nightmares.

Think on things of good report. He dragged his thoughts from the bog of guilt to what lay ahead with this investigation.

First, he'd check in with Ranger Reiger—Clay—and see what he and the officers found on the scene. He'd already texted Tucker to be on the lookout for Laurel's camera and backpack. They needed fingerprints and blood samples to see if any of it on Heath's jeans wasn't his, and he'd check with Tucker again about cameras in the Black Ash Swamp parking lot. He was pretty sure there weren't any, but he'd investigate that once he was back at the station.

Most importantly, he needed to coax Laurel into giving her statement. Her *full* statement.

Because one thing that stuck in Heath's mind like a splinter under a fingernail was Tucker mentioning Laurel's initial radio call.

"She called herself 'Ranger Campbell,' then corrected herself with 'Ranger Bell,'" Tucker had said. *Maybe she was just scared and misspoke.*

Heath's brain dialed back to their conversation a few minutes ago. Had she said "Golden Gate Trail"…? Did she mean *that* Golden Gate Bridge?

She said she was from West Virginia. Her plates confirmed that. She might've been on the West Coast for vacation, biking around the city with her dad when she was younger. Maybe she'd sprained her wrist then, had to visit a hospital. It wasn't an improbable take.

Yet he couldn't shake that Laurel Bell was hiding something. Either she knew her assailant, or she had a secret she wasn't sharing.

But why?

THREE

Laurel trailed after Molly Calhoun as they entered the Holloway Police Station later that day. Molly had already given her statement, which left Laurel to detail the awful events of the morning. The brain-muddying painkillers the nurse gave her had eased her aching body, but they'd also made her upset stomach worse. She'd been grateful for Heath's attentive care all morning, but she also had been desperate for the privacy of her own room to get cleaned up and rest a little while.

She needed to ask for a phone to call her WITSEC handler, Tim Polling. Needed to hear his reassuring voice and make sure that this was random and not connected to her dad's murder.

Her queasy stomach knotted up. What if Tim said she had to relocate?

Laurel rubbed her temples. Would she be sharp enough to fend off personal questions from Heath that she couldn't answer until speaking with Tim?

Like in the hospital waiting room. She grimaced. Had she *really* mentioned the Golden Gate Trail Loop aloud? He was easy to talk to, and it'd been too easy to let her guard down with Heath. Hopefully he would forget about that or at least not connect the dots to her old life.

Tim had been one of the few constants in a life tossed by

uncertainty, a father figure to her after she lost her adoptive parents, the Heigels. The Heigels were a compassionate older couple who had met her dad after he arrested the criminal who murdered their only son. Gary and Annaliese Heigel had repaid the favor by staying true to their promise of adopting her, despite pushing sixty when her dad was killed. Annaliese had passed away when Laurel was a college freshman, and Gary died not long after. Losing them had been a blow after everything else she'd faced in her life.

She scraped her nails across her palms. What a helpless feeling, not having her phone. It could be submerged in the swamp with her pack—unless her attacker had taken it. The other ranger who'd arrived as they left—Clay—maybe he'd found them.

A cold needle threaded her backbone. The man who attacked her might come after her again. Could he be somehow connected to August Basile? *No.* The last update she'd received from Tim said August would remain behind bars for thirty more years at the minimum, and the Basile Brotherhood, or the BB, as they were known around San Francisco, had been eradicated.

Her heavy thoughts scattered when she found herself standing in Heath Calhoun's office doorway beside Molly. He was even bigger and broader in the small space than he'd been in the hospital waiting room. With a cell to his ear, he motioned them inside. She stepped in first, but stopped short when she got a full view of Heath's face. A shiny purple half-moon encircled one eye, and another bruise stood out on his jaw.

A commotion in the hallway drew Laurel's attention, and she turned as a bear of a man with short-cropped, dark brown hair appeared. The next thing Laurel knew, he swept Molly into his arms. Molly was on the tall side, though at five foot four, lots of people were taller than Laurel. Molly's face fit into the crook of the man's neck, and they held each other for several moments.

Laurel dropped her gaze but couldn't stop her heart's yearning cry. Must be Molly's fiancé. *This* was why she adored shooting wedding pictures.

She'd often wondered what it would be like to be so close to someone that no words were needed. Just their nearness. A person who would hold her just because and not even need to say anything—they'd just calm her with their presence. Laurel returned her eyes forward and found Heath watching her, a brooding expression on his banged-up face.

She sank into one of the chairs in front of his desk.

Heath hung up then swiveled back and forth in his leather seat.

"That was Clay Reiger. He and the other officers located your bag. It was floating near one of the back ponds." He winced. "I'm sorry, but your cell is toast. Once we process the other items and check for prints, you can get them back."

Her heart sank at this news. "Any sign of my camera?"

"Oh, yeah. They found it. It must've been about where you left it when he…beforehand. The lens is cracked, but they didn't see any other external damage. Same goes. It's yours once we check for prints." Heat flooded her neck and swept into her cheeks as he scrutinized her. "Feeling better, I hope?"

"Sort of. Painkillers help this." She touched her tender throat, then her temple. "But not this." She rested her palm on her stomach.

"Ah, right. I'll take it easy about your statement." His probing hazel eyes flickered to the couple behind them. "Eli. Molly. You guys are making me sick." His tone was light, but his expression was one of focused impatience. "Laurel, this is Molly's fiancé, FBI special cyberagent Buchanan. Eli to his friends. He looks scary, but he's harmless if you're not a criminal."

Not a criminal. Laurel froze as dark memories from the day her dad was killed assailed her. Did shooting someone—even if you didn't kill them—make someone a criminal?

"It's nice to meet you." She felt foolish with all three pairs of eyes on her. It wasn't nice to be here—she'd rather be standing out in the woods photographing a fox or waterfowl or a primitive campsite as planned for the day. Anything but sitting in a police station again with an aching body, fear shadowing her and riddled with too many questions to answer.

"Would you two lovebirds fly away for a few minutes?" Heath stretched his arms above his head in a masculine display of sinew and strength, and she averted her gaze. Her photographer's eye always noted interesting subjects, shapes and colors and beauty, but Heath was most definitely not a subject she would ever explore.

"Really, Heath?" Molly blew a raspberry at her brother.

"Really. I need to go over what happened today with Ms. Bell. Take your lovey-dovies outside."

"Are you okay, Laurel?" Compassion laced Molly's voice.

I'll never really be okay. But she offered a weak nod. "Getting there."

"Thanks for keeping my girl safe." Eli saluted Heath then sent a brief nod at Laurel. "You won't find a better law enforcement officer anywhere."

Laurel worked up a weak smile in response. The two men obviously liked and respected each other.

She took in Heath's office as Molly and Eli retreated. Mostly bare except for stacks of paperwork on his desk, the space included an AA degree from a local community college on the wall and a beautiful fall picture of a huge dam—she'd guess the Holloway Dam, located near Laurel's rental cabin. A small oval picture frame sat on the table behind him, showcasing a vibrant young woman with shoulder-length brown hair hugging a little girl to her side. Both wore matching grins. They clearly adored the photographer. Heath's wife and daughter?

"You know, no one would blame you for bowing out of taking Molly and Eli's pictures this weekend." He leaned back, arms crossed over his chest. Blocking her view of the picture.

"I'll see how I feel by tomorrow, but I still would like to try." It was Tuesday, and the wedding was four days away. She couldn't tell him that after her dad's murder, and on all the anniversaries of his death after that, all she'd wanted to do was keep busy around the date. Today was no different. Knowing she had a photography shoot coming soon helped her focus on living instead of remembering. "Wedding pictures are such an optimistic occasion to shoot. It's a pleasure for me to see the joy and emotion on their faces when they commit to 'love, honor and cherish until death do them part.'"

Something painful flickered in the depths of Heath's eyes, then he looked away. What had she said wrong?

"So—" He rapped his fingers on the desk, that nervous energy resurfacing. "I ran your license, but you don't have a local address yet. It came up with Belleview Avenue, apartment twelve, in Elkins. You lived there before moving here, correct?"

"That's right." She was glad she could tell the truth for this at least. "Before that I lived in Morgantown, where I worked at a small photography studio that takes class pictures for elementary schools while I was getting my degree at WVU. It… took me a while to finish."

"Hey, at least you did it. And after getting your degree, you were employed by the US Forest Service there in West Virginia for three years?"

"Yes, at Monongahela National Forest."

He rested the eraser on his chin, contemplating her in an unnerving way that she was coming to realize was Heath Calhoun's normal mode of operating. Direct, but not cruel. Focused, but not aloof. No, he didn't threaten her in the least. In fact, she felt completely safe with him. It was a strangely welcoming sensation, but it also put her on edge. Tim had made it clear to contact him immediately should any unusual situations arise. Sharing her past, with her dad's murder and her life in WITSEC, would put her and others in danger.

Laurel grasped the end of her braid and coiled a finger around the elastic piece holding it in place that Molly offered earlier. She had to find a way to call Tim.

"Would it be possible to make a call on one of the phones at the station?"

"Of course. You can use the landline when we finish up." Heath took a swig from a coffee mug on his desk that said Steelers. "You want anything to drink before we get started?"

"No, thanks." *Just a chance to make a phone call.*

"Okay." He pulled out a notepad and mechanical pencil from his top drawer. "Let's start at the beginning. I need to know what happened at the swamp before Molly and I arrived. Be as detailed as possible, and I understand you're on medication so take your time."

His sensitivity to her leftover brain fog and upset stomach was appreciated, but it didn't alleviate the slower-than-normal rate at which she recalled those terrible events, and the fight-or-flight reaction her body had when she went over what happened earlier today. She started speaking, then stopped, her heart thudding as she attempted to describe when her attacker appeared and what he looked like. Heath scribbled furiously, and she focused on the spot where his large hand gripped the pencil. During the part where her attacker dragged her toward the water, the room blurred.

The writing utensil stilled, and his brows folded together. "If you need to take a breather, we have a couch in the break room. I can clear it out first."

Again, the urge to plead for a phone nearly took over her tongue.

"No, thank you." She just needed to get this over with. "When the man pushed me under, over and over, I thought…" A tear traced her cheek, and he lifted a tissue box from his desk and handed it to her. "I thought that was it."

"You're safe now." Heath's features were carved in granite, but his eyes remained soft. "You know that, right?"

"I've never been safe." The jagged words slipped out like doves freed from a cage.

"I'm sorry?"

She waved her fingers and sniffled. "Never mind, it's nothing. Can we keep going with my statement?"

"Sure. Let's talk about what you heard. Did he speak to you? Could you identify his voice?"

"He barely spoke. He seemed…intent. Really, really focused. Emotionless." She pictured his masked face and calculated actions, then flinched.

"So, nothing about his build, movement or voice was familiar?"

She shook her head, her mouth bone dry.

Heath reclined in the chair, staring up at the ceiling for a few moments. When he dropped his chin and met her eyes, there was an unshakable resolve in them. "I will do everything in my power to make sure he never hurts you again."

Tears stung her throat. "Thank you."

Several seconds passed as she grabbed another tissue to dab her face.

"I'm curious—which subject do you enjoy taking pictures of more, people or animals?"

Was this a distraction? "Well, that depends on the animal and the person and the day. Some days I enjoy the solitude of documenting the courting ritual of cardinals, while other times I found the laughter of a second grader refusing to take a picture without his tongue sticking out is just what I needed."

Heath snorted. "Guess there's positives and negatives to both. Do you mind me asking whereabouts you're living now? I didn't catch the address."

The second abrupt change of topic jarred her. "I rented a small cabin on Tawny Ridge, near the dam. It's a six-month rental, then I was going to see about buying options if the market improved and if the job here works out."

"Ah. Okay. Close to the ranger headquarters." A look of concern crossed his face. "You're kind of by yourself up there."

The man missed nothing. "I like the solitude."

"I get it." He sat forward, his chair squeaking as he dropped his elbows to the desk. "After a long day, there's nothing I need more than going home and crashing with my little girl. Shutting out the world. Watching a movie or playing Battleship."

"My dad and I used to play Battleship when he was off work." She sank in the chair, longing to rewind the words. Bringing up her dad right now was a bad idea. Heath needed to know as little about her as possible. Until she spoke with Tim, she had to keep her past under wraps.

Heath heaved out a sigh and held her gaze. "So, in this line of work, instinct is often a guide. A warning sensor when there's an issue in the engine I can't actually see, if you will.

And my instinct is telling me there's more information here you haven't told me."

How did he know? She willed her breathing slower. Measured.

"Your instinct must be wrong." Her muscles quaked, and she looked down. If he found out about her WITSEC placement, she would have to leave this beautiful area and her dream job.

"Ms. Bell. I apologize for being so forward, but—"

"Laurel. Just call me Laurel, please." It was the only piece left of her former life, just a portion of her old name, but she clung to it like a child to the edges of a slippery slide.

"*Laurel.* The last thing I want to do is pressure you or cause you more distress today. I'm on your side. And I want to catch the man who did this to you. But to do so, I need your complete honesty. All the cards on the table."

"I don't play cards."

He lifted one broad shoulder. "I don't either, really. Just UNO with Piper."

Fire lit her limbs, and she stood. "I need to make a call, please."

He held out his hand, and Laurel sank to the chair, her chest rising and falling quickly. Too quickly. Did he notice?

"I'll let you make a phone call, but may I ask a couple more questions first?"

She nodded slowly. What else could she say?

"Do you have an ex who is after you? A boyfriend or husband?"

"No." At least she could answer that truthfully. She'd barely dated because of what happened all those years ago. Trusting a man other than her dad, Gary Heigel or Tim Polling felt risky. Frightening. She'd made a couple male friends in college, and there'd been definite interest for a romantic relationship, but she'd shut those doors immediately.

"Alright. Second question. You were in the middle of a National Forest, in a swamp. Finding you must've been a challenge. Yet this man did and came after you with the intent to kill. Do you have any idea why?"

All her life, trouble had followed her and her family. While August Basile was in jail, could there be someone else—a person who knew him—after her now?

Had another man survived the police-led purge of the Basile Brotherhood, and he was coming after her now?

She shook her head and stared at her lap. "I'm sorry, I don't know why."

Heath led her to the community room tucked at the back of the station. The long, narrow space had a rectangular table that fit almost all their staff during weekly meetings along with a couple computers set up on tables against the wall. Four additional folding chairs were stacked in a corner, and several plaques and awards dotted the white walls. A lone window relieved the room of its shadows.

He flicked the lights on as they entered. The goal was to get more information out of this skittish woman without pressuring her, and this might be the way to do it. What he hadn't disclosed to her was that he'd called Tucker Brindley, her supervisor with the Forest Service, and requested he send over copies of her application. The investigation into her attack raised questions—and she'd been vague enough so far—that it qualified for a full background check.

Too bad her application stated that she grew up in West Virginia. Nothing new. Yet in the hospital she'd mentioned the Golden Gate something…trail? Maybe there was a Golden Gate Trail in West Virginia. He'd check on that later.

While Heath preferred to interview victims in his office to set an easygoing tone between him and the person or people, Laurel still hadn't revealed all she knew. She didn't seem an obstinate person by nature, or dishonest, so there must be a reason. There had to be something about this perp she didn't want to share. But why the secrecy?

In order to break through that wall, he had one of his officers pull up several images of criminals that best matched the physical description of the man he'd sparred with at Black Ash Swamp. They'd printed out eight-by-tens for Laurel to examine. Heath was no lightweight, and this man had been formidably built. In the quick flashes of limbs Heath had seen, it appeared her attacker was dark-haired, as per the glimpse of thick forearm hair Heath had gotten. Maybe seeing these mug shots would jog her memory and help her admit her connection to the criminal who attacked her.

Heath stepped into the room behind Laurel. She wore black leggings and a blue Canoe the Allegheny T-shirt Molly had brought to the hospital earlier. Her petite frame swam in the shirt, and the end of her long, braided hair was still twined around her pointer finger.

Nervous habit. He had a few of those.

"What are those pictures?" She looked down at the conference table, bare except for the mug shots taken in the last year and a leftover coffee mug from their last meeting. The criminals fit the basic description he gave his officer—around five-eleven to six foot, 195-plus. Dark hair, muscular build. Wanted for other crimes in the northeastern US, particularly West Virginia and Pennsylvania.

"Mug shots." He pulled out a chair and motioned for her to sit. Finally she did, her lips ajar and body stiff.

"I know you didn't see your attacker's face, but do any of

these guys look like they could match the physical build of the perp who came after you today?"

He paced around the table to give her space as she fingered through the photographs. Then she exhaled and pushed the stack away from her.

"Are all these criminals from Pennsylvania?"

"Pennsylvania and West Virginia for the most part." He edged closer, recalling when he was ten years old and trying to feed the orphaned fawn his dad rescued beside its dead mother on the roadside. His dad had captured it, folded it carefully in a blanket, set the fawn in the back of their old Ford Explorer and driven home with the baby deer days before Christmas. As the oldest of four kids, he'd taken charge of the animal, making a little home for it in their garden shed out back. A blanket fort for protection, because of course a baby deer needed a fort. Molly had helped some, too. He'd figured out what they ate—their mother's milk, of course—and his mom had purchased some type of canned animal milk, then helped him prepare a bottle. For forty-eight hours, Heath stayed in the shed, trying to get the fawn to warm up to him. He'd cared for and finally fed it despite the animal's initial fear of him. Christmas Eve morning he'd put on a brave face when a kindly worker from a wild animal rescue arrived to take her away. Then he'd gone to his room and cried for an hour, wishing for more time for the baby deer to learn to love him the way he had immediately loved the spindly-legged little creature.

Spot. The fawn's name came back now, all these years ago.

"Sergeant Calhoun?"

Her soft voice drew him back to the present. Laurel Bell was no fawn. She was a grown woman, rather attractive if he was being honest with himself, though he needed to forget that fact and treat her like any other crime victim. With respect and caution.

"Yes?" He blinked at her.

"I just… I didn't see him." She held his eyes. "I'm sorry."

Hope sparked at the hesitation he saw in her blue-rimmed brown gaze. She wanted to share something. What kept her from doing so?

He pulled out the chair beside her, rolled it back, then sat. Facing her, he leaned down, elbows to knees. Patient despite his impatience. "I know today has been traumatic for you," he began, noting how her eyes glazed over. Not a good beginning. Backing up and starting again. "You were tough out there."

Her mouth tightened. "I ran away. I had to."

Shoving aside his hesitation, he clasped then cradled her slender hands in his. "Laurel, you were fighting for your life."

She whispered a single word that sounded like *again*, but he ignored it and continued.

"I very much want to help you find the man who tried to kill you." He gulped, surprised at two things. First, she didn't pull away from his careful touch, and second, she seemed to be softening.

Which meant they were closer to finding this scumbag who went after her. It had to be an ex-husband or ex-boyfriend, even though she had denied it earlier. Maybe a narcissist who wanted to kill her so no one else could have her either. He'd seen the scenario before, and it sickened him.

He would forgive her for lying earlier about it not being her ex. She'd been scared, under duress.

"Take your time."

"It's not that." She shook her head.

Heath felt like they were so close to a breakthrough. So close to the truth. He cleared his throat. "When I was younger, our golden retriever Dusty cornered this squirrel in the garage. That little thing climbed everywhere he could, but of course there was a roof and doors and glass panes, and he couldn't get out. Dusty probably wouldn't have killed it, but the squirrel didn't know that. When I finally shooed Dusty into the house, got a big towel and contained the little thing, I realized it was a young one. Its eyes were huge, and it looked so terrified as I carried it outside, past our fenced yard so it would have a fighting chance again. I don't know how else to say it, but that little squirrel looked terrified and tired. Like it had been chased for days, or weeks." He hesitated. "I see that in your eyes, too."

"Please." She pulled her hands from his and pushed her chair away until it crashed into the chair beside it. "I need to make that phone call."

Laurel averted her face, but not before he noted the telltale gleam of tears. Leaving his hands cold and his thoughts churning, her reaction confirmed what he believed to be the truth about this attack.

Laurel had been chased just like that little squirrel. But by whom? And why wouldn't she tell him?

The question that plagued him now, was who was she so desperate to call?

FOUR

Laurel couldn't look at Heath. Couldn't be close. Couldn't let his sweet story about the scared squirrel and the dog sink in too deeply. His uncanny ability to see through her was unnerving. Frightening. Of all the people she could've met, why this astute, doggedly determined police officer—who also happened to be handsome?

Heath leaned back in the chair and roped his long, muscular arms behind his head. He stared up at the conference room ceiling, and she took the opportunity to quickly catalog his features. A slightly oversize, masculine nose, strong jaw covered by a trimmed brown beard, hazel eyes the color of trees just budding to life in spring and short brown hair tinted with auburn. His ease in carrying her earlier was a testament to his rangy build and lean musculature.

A photographic scene formed in her mind's eye. Heath in uniform, leaning against his truck. That confident, mischievous gleam in his eye.

Stop it, Laurel. She rubbed a hand across her face. *He might be good-looking, but he's just another cop, and maybe a dirty one at that.*

No, that wasn't fair. She was almost certain Heath Calhoun *wasn't* dirty. The honorable and caring way he'd treated her, even when she was at her worst, spoke more about his character than a hundred boasts.

But she knew it still wasn't wise to tell him her entire story. She'd hate for something to happen to him or his family because of her.

"I asked our receptionist to get you a burner phone," Heath noted. "You can use that or the landline to call."

"Thank you." She pressed her lips together and chanced a look his way.

"I'm sorry to drag this out. I thought these mug shots might jog your memory a bit."

"I know you're just trying to do your job." A thought struck. "When we're done, I'd like to go back to my place and rest. My head is pounding."

"That leads me to the next order of business. We have another little problem."

"I'd say I have quite a few *big* problems."

He gave her a grim smile that didn't last long. "With your attacker on the loose, I don't think it's a good idea that you're alone. That includes at your cabin."

"Where does that leave me?" She twined her hands on the table, her voice rising and all her frazzled nerves pinpointing her focus on him. "Do I sleep here at the station then?"

He took in her sudden outburst with a calm, measured expression that further incensed her. Her eyes stung. One tiny, logical brain cell recognized his patient demeanor was part of why he was an excellent police officer. But right now, with her brain fog, stomach sketchy and her body aching all over, she wasn't going to listen to that stubborn brain cell.

"Please stop acting like everything is a-okay when someone just tried to kill me." Laurel cupped her palms over her face. She'd never spoken so rudely to a near stranger, and heat burned her middle. If only there was a hole in the laminate floor into which she could disappear.

"How about I go with you to the cabin so you're not alone?"

"I just met you. And while you helped me today and your sister adores you, that doesn't mean I want you at my cabin. What about your wife and daughter?"

He recoiled, then his face returned to a blank slate. She sagged as her father's voice thundered through her mind from when she was eight and a half and she yelled at a friend on the playground who wouldn't do what Laurel told her to do. *I know you miss your mom, Lauralee Campbell, but that doesn't mean you get to be rude to others or tell them what to do. Don't feel sorry for yourself, and don't hurt others when you're hurting. Love is kind. And patient. Not rude.*

Patience had never been a virtue of hers, as much as her dad attempted to drum it into her, but apparently Heath had it in abundance.

"I'll work those details out." His mouth tightened. "Back to my original point. I do not believe it's wise or prudent that you're alone out there. The cabin is six miles from the station and two miles from the nearest fire department."

"I'm not helpless," she muttered.

"I didn't say you were. You seem like an independent and capable woman. But when a criminal like that has their mind made up..." His throat bobbed on a swallow.

"I don't want to put you, Molly or your family out any more than I already have."

"They're not coming after *my* family. The man came after you. Do you *want* to be by yourself tonight?" he asked bluntly.

"Yes. No." She threw her hands out. "I'm not sure what I want. The plan was to start a new life here, leave my past behind and actually live. Live, without worrying about—"

She cut off her words. So close. She was so close to revealing too much.

"About that man coming after you?"

He believed she knew her attacker. Well, that much wasn't true, but she did wonder if it was a criminal connected to the Basile Brotherhood. To August Basile. But that couldn't be. He'd been behind bars for years, and no one had come after her yet.

Laurel deflated at the compassion in his eyes. Why was she reacting so strongly to him helping her? Shame licked her skin, drawing heat up into her cheeks. "I'm sorry. I don't know what's wrong with me. I was taught better manners than this." Her dad would be ashamed of her behavior toward Heath. "I'm being a porcupine."

"You're protecting yourself."

"Stop being so reasonable!" She glared at him, only to find one of his thick brows cocked, a tiny grin on his face. It was physically and emotionally impossible not to smile back.

"I'll cut that out right now."

"Good. Thank you." How had he made her smile when she was about to cry? "I'm nervous that I won't be alert because of the effects of the pain medication, so yes. You're right, it's probably best I'm not alone."

"That happened with Kara, too." His eyelids flickered as he looked past Laurel. "My wife. When she had our daughter, Piper, she had a C-section. The pain meds…" A nostalgic expression pulled at his features. "She called it being 'foggy-brained.' She hated it."

His wife's name is Kara. "Yes, same. I don't feel like I can think straight."

A knock came from the conference room door, and a middle-aged woman poked her head inside. "Here you go, Sergeant."

"Thanks." Heath accepted the phone, then handed the

nondescript black cell to Laurel. Her heart leaped. "We also have a landline here at the station, if you'd prefer to call out on that."

"This will work. Thank you."

"You…know the number?"

By heart. Tim had her memorize it years ago. "I do." She hesitated. "Would you mind if I…have some privacy?"

"Sure." He stood then rounded the far edge of the table. "Let me know when you're done."

"I will." She snatched the phone, afraid he'd change his mind.

Heath strode to the door, leaving her alone with her thoughts and the plain little phone.

She pulled up the dial pad, tapped in Tim's number then pressed the green button. It rang eight times…ten…thirteen then went to voicemail.

His voicemail box recording began. "This is Tim. Leave me a message. If it's an emergency, you can reach my Director, Alex Vegas at…" She waited for the beep, her thoughts racing, then began stuttering out what happened. "Tim. It's LB." He was one of the few people alive who knew her real name, but he'd taught her to use her initials even in voicemails. "Someone attacked me today. Not August. Someone else. I don't know who. Please, call me back. I'm…okay. The local police department in Holloway is taking care of me. I can't say anything to them, right?" She sniffled, longing for more time to explain. Longing to hear his familiar, steady voice. "Anyway, I need to know what you want me to do. Call me back on this number, please."

Laurel clicked end then blinked up at the popcorn ceiling. Would Heath let her keep this phone until she got hers back? Why was everything so complicated?

A normal life. Peace. The comfort of a routine. A hug each day. Someone to love her and for her to love them back. That was all she wanted.

But first she had to deal with this day. This moment. Heath would accompany her back to her cabin, where a small mountain of unpacked boxes took over the living room and spilled into her bedroom. She pressed the knuckles of her free hand to her forehead, warding off a pounding headache. Why it mattered what her living space looked like to Heath Calhoun, she wasn't sure.

She shouldn't care.

But he cared, and that's *why* it mattered. Living under witness protection had taught her many things, the least of which was how to judge the sincerity of a person's words by their actions. While she'd just met Heath, already he'd proven he had her best interest at heart and only wanted to help.

Laurel's spine sagged, and she leaned into the conference table. Would she ever truly be able to let anyone in, other than her dad, her WITSEC handlers and the Heigels?

She squared her shoulders, opened the door and entered the hallway. Voices carried down from the front desk. As she approached Heath's office, she slowed, peeking inside. He reclined in his chair, gripping the photo frame she'd seen earlier—the one with his wife and daughter. Stark emotion covered his face, stopping her short.

Sadness? Grief?

She inched back quietly so he wouldn't know she'd been standing there staring, but he must've sensed her presence. His chair squeaked violently as he straightened, and the picture was gone, placed facedown on the desk before Laurel blinked.

"Did you reach anyone?"

She stepped inside his office. "No, it went to his voicemail." She gripped the phone. "Can I…may I keep this phone, since my cell was damaged? I need to talk to him—to this person, and how will I know if he calls back?"

He regarded her with an aloof expression, but instinct told her he was measuring her words, each and every one. Maybe he thought she was calling a boyfriend or significant other?

Finally, he spoke. "You can keep the phone, but at some point, I need to know everything—and everyone—involved with and about this situation."

I can't. While Heath Calhoun was her ally now, and she had no choice but to place her life in his hands, he and his beautiful family could end up in danger if she revealed who she really was. And she wouldn't let that happen.

Heath accepted the white fast-food bag from the drive-through window and said *thank you* to the distracted teenager tossing it his way. He peered around the bustling parking lot, his gaze fast and furious as he looked for a quiet spot to eat. Holloway wasn't a very big town, and when he was off duty, he wanted to be off the social grid as well.

Laurel stared out the window, watching as a mom holding a little girl herded two rambunctious boys into a silver SUV, the two boys pretending to fly the airplane toys from the kids' meals. Mundane moments in life, and yet they felt so out of reach for him. Glimpses of days gone by, when Kara, Piper and he would grab burgers here and drive over to Sylvan Park, right off the river, and eat on the picnic bench while Piper entertained them with stories about princess ballerinas becoming pirates and fighting the bad guys, then running off her energy with the other kids at the playground.

"Would you like to eat here—" he gestured at several outdoor tables under bright red canopies "—or in the car?"

She finally turned to face him. "I wouldn't mind some sunlight and fresh air."

Her answer pleased him, because he'd been craving the same thing. A few moments outside. Leaving walls and worries behind. Well, most of them. He'd need to keep his guard up at all times.

Heath parked, then they climbed out and headed toward one of the empty tables. He reached into the bag and handed her the box with her chicken tenders, side of coleslaw and her bottled water, then dug his items out.

"Do you mind if I bless the food?" he asked.

Her eyes widened. "Okay." He stole an assessing glance around before bowing his head.

"Dear God, we ask You to bless this food You've provided. We ask for Your protection over Laurel and for answers about her case. Keep our families safe, please. Amen."

"Amen," she echoed. "Thank you. That was nice."

"My dad's a pastor. Whenever we eat, we pray."

"I think that must be the glue that binds families' faith together." She sipped her water. "Not that I'm an expert at anything faith-related. I'm still…struggling with mine."

"Same here." He took a bite of his burger, regretting the size of it as he chewed around the food and considered her comment. What happened that she struggled with her faith? He definitely still struggled. Still clung to that residual anger that God had allowed Kara to slip from this life to the next with Him, when Heath and Piper needed her here so much.

The overlarge bite fell like a stone into his gut.

Two gray schnauzers raced by with their owners. The foursome headed to a small SUV, where the couple loaded the small dogs in the back seat.

"I'd like to have a dog one day." She nibbled on a tender.

Heath noted the longing in her voice. "You are welcome to dog-sit Axel and Forge any day of the week. Though they are a bit of a handful at times."

"What kind of dogs do you have?"

"Axel is a German shepherd and Forge is a Dutch shepherd. They're both retired K-9 officers. Fierce and family-oriented. They love all the belly rubs they can get."

"Two big dogs, huh?" A natural smile graced her face, and the transformation stole his breath. "That fits about what I'd expect."

"Maybe I'm scared of Chihuahuas." He set the last bite of his burger down, and they chuckled together. "Axel and Forge love Piper. One sleeps with me, the other stays with Piper. He's devastated she's gone."

Her smile tanked. "What do you mean, she's gone?"

"She's at her grandparents' in Hershey."

"Do you miss her?"

"Every second. But she needs to spend time with them. It helps with…" He slammed his mouth shut and scratched the back of his neck. Enough of that. She didn't need to know that he was widowed. *Keep your personal lives separate from your work lives*, Chief Lane reminded their team at the HPD from time-to-time. *Makes life easier if they don't mix.*

She finished the tender then picked up a fork to dig into her coleslaw. "Do they have a backyard to run around in?"

"Sure do. We have one and a half acres fenced. My sister Katie works from home and when I'm logging in long hours or working on a case, she goes over, takes care of Piper if she's off school and throws the ball for the dogs."

"Does your wife work long hours, too?"

"No. Kara…taught school before she had Piper, but we worked out our finances, so she was able to stay home when Piper was little." He tossed his fries back in the bag and stood.

"Heath?" She tilted her head. "What's wrong?"

"Nothing. You done?"

"Yes." She handed off her containers, and he pitched the

food in a nearby trash can, keeping Laurel in his peripheral vision. Hopefully it was a polite enough way to stop the direction of this conversation.

He surveyed the busy area, returning his focus to their situation. So far, there'd been nothing suspicious at the fast-food restaurant, although a couple vehicles had slowed near his truck because the drive-through line had grown. He didn't want to spend any more time here than necessary.

He motioned. "You about ready to go?"

She nodded then they walked to his truck. He gave the vehicle a quick once-over, and they climbed inside and headed back onto the main road. When he put the cabin's address into the map app, it said four miles. His goal was to arrive with plenty of daylight to spare.

The interior of the vehicle felt stuffy as they drove away from the restaurant, so he clicked up the a/c. His gaze ping-ponged from the road in front to the rearview mirror, and he and Laurel rode in companiable silence for a couple of minutes.

"So, what kind of dog would you get if you could choose one?" he asked because he was genuinely curious.

"I don't really care what kind. I'd probably adopt the oldest, neediest one. The dog that looked the most lost. They deserve love as much as the young, energetic ones."

"Absolutely." He exhaled. "I'd like to adopt another one, but right now we can only handle those two goofballs."

A dinging sound emitted from his dashboard, and a red light blinked just below the speedometer. Heath scowled. One of his tires had low pressure.

The steering wheel jerked slightly, and he firmed his grip while scouting for a spot to pull over. They were still a couple of miles from her cabin. Trees hugged the roadside, and clouds gathered overhead as the sun escaped the sky on the western horizon. A quarter mile to their left, the Allegheny River carved through the terrain, a glittering blue-gray snake in the fading light. All the beauty of this area he loved was lost on him as realization seared into reality.

These were new tires. Had he run over a nail, or had someone tampered with them, either at the station or when his attention was on Laurel at the restaurant?

"Why are we slowing down?"

"I need to check my tires. Looks like one might be flat." Heath spotted an area that would afford them a bit of cover while getting his formidable truck all the way off the road. The Rainbow Falls parking lot.

He drove slowly on the softening tire, the truck leaning low on the left side, then clicked on his blinker and turned in. Huh. No other cars here. He jammed his shifter into Park and unbuckled, grabbing his phone to shoot off a text to Eli.

"Did we hit something?" she asked.

"Not sure. We either ran over glass I didn't see back there, or my tire was compromised."

"Compromised?" She gaped at him.

"Tampered with. On purpose." Now to get the spare on quickly and get them out of here.

Because his gut was telling him Laurel's attacker wasn't far behind.

FIVE

Laurel huddled in the truck as Heath inspected his tire. He had been right at the station. Her cabin *was* remote, and the thought of staying out here in the woods—alone—after what happened today at the swamp sent sparks through her nerves.

She sat up, peering out into the fading daylight. Heath crouched near the driver-side front tire. When he stood, he let out a long, slow whistle.

"You have got to be kidding me." He circled the truck, laying his arm on the open window. "Someone laid out some pretty hefty nails at the police station or the restaurant. There are at least three in my front left tire." He wiped a trail of grimy sweat from his brow. "I'm surprised we got as far as we did."

"Has Eli texted or called you back?"

Heath dug his cell from his jeans' pocket. "Not yet. He might be in a meeting, or driving."

Her mouth felt like it had been stuffed with cotton balls. A thick line of trees hedged them in on both sides of the road, blocking out the scant remaining sunlight. It would be dark soon. A tremble started in her middle and worked out to her limbs. She'd driven back and forth from Holloway to her cabin several times since arriving, but it had always been during daylight.

And she hadn't just been attacked.

"Where are we?" She opened the door and climbed out of the truck to stand beside him.

"Near Rainbow Falls, which means your cabin is about two miles northeast, thataway." He pointed. "Not too far from the dam, but unfortunately not close to much else. I better get the spare out." He started toward the back of the truck.

The sound of a car engine turned them both around. At the top of the hill they'd just crested, a vehicle appeared. Dark blue or black, an older SUV, it traveled at a high rate of speed toward them. Its headlights were off despite the veil of darkness descending in the area.

Heath's cell rang, and he jabbed the screen. "Calhoun here."

"You rang. What's up?" Eli's voice.

Laurel sidled up next to him, staring at the approaching SUV. Her heart rate jumped into overdrive.

"Eli, we have a 10-33."

"Location?" Eli demanded.

A whining noise flew past her head. In one fluid movement, Heath wrapped his arm around her then dived to the ground beside the truck. Grit and tiny pebbles scratched her arms as they skidded, but he took the brunt of the fall. His cell phone bounced from his hand, skidding across the gravel and landing beneath the bed of his truck.

"Is that the driver shooting at us?" she cried.

"The passenger is. We need to get out of here. Can you run?"

"I…yes." She was breathless, her head spinning. Her burner phone was still in the car. What if Tim called her back? "The phone is in the—"

"No time." Heath lifted her upright then hauled her toward the tree line as the approaching car's engine roared closer.

"We have to run to the right. See over there? That's the trail leading to the fall. Don't go that way. It's too slippery and dangerous to run in that area." Heath pointed, then pressed his palm to her lower back. "If something happens, keep running. Find a spot to hide."

"Wait—the cell—"

"Laurel. They will kill you. Move!" He pushed her forward, and they darted to the right like he told her, each stride sending another fearful question through her mind.

Where would they go, and how would Tim reach her now?

The vehicle's engine noise increased, then cut off. Silence followed, with only their frantic footsteps among the pine needles and ferns. One slam sounded, echoing into the woods after her and Heath like a warning. The second slam sent liquid fire through her veins.

"They're out of the car," Heath panted.

The scent of pine needles and dirt clung to her nose as they stumbled onward, slowed down by the rocks and hilly landscape. Ferns grabbed their legs and blue jays protested overhead.

"They're in the woods, too. Keep going!" Heath shouted from behind as they zigzagged through the trees. She hoisted herself over a boulder the size of a cow and slid down its damp, mossy back side. When she landed, her shoe snagged on a chunk of rock, flinging her forward.

Heath caught her just before she face-planted, hefting her upright. Then he half carried, half dragged her forward until she found her footing. Twilight dressed the treetops, and the forest's lighting dimmed, setting the sky ablaze with coral flames. Her photographer's eye noted the beauty, even for just one heart-racing moment, and she whispered a prayer.

God please, get us away from them. Keep us safe.

"Hang a left here. This way." He headed to the left, and she hurried after him as they continued to ascend the stony hillside. The dim rush of water sounded nearby. Must be the falls. The trees thinned out, and he slowed to check their progress.

They panted, trying to catch their breath. Heath drew her down and turned, inspecting the woods. "I don't see them… but I can hear them." His rough whisper sent alarm bells clanging in her head.

"Maybe they went toward the falls."

"Wait—they're behind that cluster of trees downhill. Move!"

He pushed her forward, using his hand to let her know when to change directions and correcting her trajectory. Each stride stretched her sore muscles, and her throat burned as more questions plagued her.

"Did you…get your phone?" she gasped out.

"It's under my truck. No chance." His voice brooked no doubt about how much that bothered him. "Eli will come for us."

But what if the men followed them or waited them out before he arrived? She pushed aside her worries as they scrambled over stumps and rocks. The ground leveled out, then they took another left. Her heart rate increased as the terrain steepened again, the treacherous landscape limiting their progress. "Do you…know where we're going?"

"Rimrock. It's a hiking area…that overlooks the dam and river. Your cabin is past the dam, to the north."

A painful swell of gratitude welled up, stinging her throat and eyes. If she'd been alone right now…she might be dead. The men certainly would've caught her. Instead, she was with Heath, who knew the area well and seemed to guess just when she was about to collapse. His steadying hand kept finding her elbows to stabilize her.

"I'm here." He spoke near her ear. "We'll get away from them."

"Can you stop…reading my mind, please?"

He clicked his tongue. "Your shoulders droop when you start to slow down," he explained. "I'm sorry, but right now we can't risk stopping or slowing down."

"The men are still back there?"

He hesitated for so long she turned to look at him. "For our safety, I'm assuming yes."

They plugged on, their pace decreasing as they scaled the small mountain leading them to Rimrock. She'd heard the name but hadn't yet visited this area. Up ahead, several huge boulders loomed like pirate ships run aground.

"People climb on these?"

"Absolutely. I've been climbing and hiking out here since I was a kid." He paused, chest heaving. "I asked Kara to marry me on the lookout above."

She jerked her head up at this revelation. "Was she expecting it? The proposal?"

"Not really." She turned, catching a ghost of a smile on his face as he spoke. "We had a family party two days later, for the Fourth of July. I think she wondered if I'd propose then, under the fireworks." He shook his head. "I wanted to surprise her, and I did. She loved it. Cried, whooped it up. A couple hikers came over because they were worried about her." He chuckled. "I used to tease her that she didn't have a volume button. When she was happy, everyone knew it."

"What a sweet memory." Her heart expanded, filling with warmth but also a tingle of longing. She wasn't sure she'd ever have that, have a man go out of his way to surprise her and who would care so deeply about her. "I'm sorry my situation has taken you away from them and put you in danger."

He waved his hand. "It's part of my job."

"You said your daughter—Piper—is with your in-laws. Is Kara there, too?"

He stumbled over the lip of a wide stone, then halted, wiping the back of his hand across his brow. "Kara died a couple years ago."

Shock spread in her vision like dark clouds before a storm. "Heath, I didn't realize… I shouldn't have asked about—"

"You didn't know."

"What happened?" She spoke aloud before she thought better about her question.

"Kara was a Division I soccer player. In great shape, athletic. But there was a family history of heart problems, and she didn't know she had LVNC—left ventricular noncompaction cardiomyopathy—until it was too late." He jammed a hand through his hair. "She was…expecting when she died. The doctors think the second pregnancy weakened her heart and…"

"I am so sorry." She set her palm on his forearm. It corded beneath her touch, warm skin reminding her that Heath might be a tough, resourceful man, but he was also human and shattered from the loss of his wife. Maybe not physically broken, but she heard the anguish in his voice. Saw the regret gleaming from his eyes.

"Thank you. It was really hard. Piper was pretty lost for a couple months. Slept with me, followed me around. That's part of why we adopted the retired K-9s. Protection and comfort."

"I can tell you're a great dad."

"Yeah, well, if only I'd been a better husband," he mumbled, then resumed hiking uphill.

Leaving Laurel to wonder what he meant.

Heath urged Laurel toward the top of Rimrock. They were both gasping for air by the time they reached the trail area. Darkness cloaked the forest, and a bad taste filled his mouth.

Why had he told her about Kara? Laurel was caring, and easy to talk to, but she was dealing with her own problems and didn't need to add his sob story to her current struggles. It had been a breach of professionalism.

"From this vantage point, I can see and hear if and when they follow us." He pointed at a house-sized boulder lodged into the top of the hill. A fissure split down the middle of it. "There's a narrow cave in between. For now, let's hunker down inside. Wait them out."

"Do you think we're going to be out here all night?"

"I hope not, but I want to prepare for that in case." He guided her a few more steps uphill until they stood just below the cave's opening. "The plan is to get back to the truck if possible."

They clambered up the remaining steps until the cave was only a few yards above them. Heath rubbed his palms together. "I hope you're not scared of dark, tight spaces."

"I love them," she said, deadpan, and he stopped, eyeing her.

"Right. Me, too." Heath snorted as they scaled the crooked, uneven stone steps. Laurel had a sense of humor lurking beneath the surface that surprised and pleased him. What would it have been like if they'd met under different circumstances? If he hadn't pulled her from the murky swamp and—

Knock it off, Calhoun.

He reached a level spot just below the entrance and slowed. They were hemmed in by huge boulders that formed as natural walls, and any person reaching the mouth of the cave would make considerable noise. He should be able to hear anyone approach. Still, a frisson of unease surged down his spine.

He patted his weapon, holstered on his hip. For now, no backup. And only one weapon, against two men who were both likely well-armed. Sweat gathered on his temples.

"Is there another way out of the cave?" she asked.

"Not really. There's a smaller area at the back, kind of like a hidden chamber, but I can't fit inside. You might be able to."

When she turned, they stood only a few inches apart. Because he was on a lower rock, they were nearly face-to-face. Even in the fading twilight, he noticed a rainbow of emotions—fear, worry, gratitude—flickering in her eyes as she regarded him.

Heath dropped his gaze. What was wrong with him?

"I'll go first and take the hit with the spiderwebs." He clasped her elbow and helped her up the last steep section at the cave's mouth.

"Whoa, it looks really narrow in there."

"It gets wider the deeper inside you go." But he didn't want to lie to her. "It'll be uncomfortable. But this will work to our advantage if the men don't see it. We can hide out in here until they pass by or head back to their car."

Heath scrambled past her to get to the opening. He wasn't sure of the cave's exact size, but it couldn't be more than six or eight feet at the widest section, maybe nine or ten feet high, and tapered down near the back.

"It's cold in here." She rubbed her forearms.

"There's a constant flow of cooler air, even in the summer." Heath inspected the insides, testing the chilly stone walls and kicking at the dark corners in case furry rodents were about. At the back of the cave, where it was narrowest, Heath attempted to wedge himself between the thick, flat rocks, only to stop halfway because his shoulders and chest wouldn't fit.

She edged up next to him. "That's the hidden chamber?"

"Yeah." He carefully moved around her, then found a low boulder near the opening and sank onto it. "You want to see if you can fit?"

She slipped through fairly easily then disappeared. After a few seconds he called out to make sure she wasn't stuck.

"Laurel, you okay?"

"Sorry, I'm here." She burst back through, bumping into his legs. He stood, helped steady her, then let go of her warm arm quickly. "That would be a lot more fun if it wasn't dark and there weren't men after us. Also, if I had my camera."

"Yeah, well, maybe one day I'll bring you up here again to take pictures. Right now, I'm going to stay by the entrance to keep an ear out."

She picked her way around the tight space, then ended up beside him on the low, long stone.

"How long do we wait in here?" she whispered.

"As long as it takes to be sure we're not going to be ambushed when we go back to my truck."

She pondered that for several minutes. When his impatience won, Heath broke the silence. "Do you know who's coming after you, Laurel?"

On the hike here, he'd shared too much about himself. Shared things about Kara's death he hadn't even disclosed to his sisters, which felt almost like a peace deal with Laurel. Would she offer any details about her past in return?

Heath closed his eyes as the mossy, dank smell burned his nose and the faraway hoot of an owl stretched inside the cave. Laurel sat still as a statue beside him, her breathing the only sound. *Nothing.* Finally, he sighed. If she wouldn't share what she was up against, or at least what she knew about her attacker, then it would be difficult to keep her safe.

"Heath, please believe me… I'm not sure who is coming after me. But I can promise it's not an ex-boyfriend or husband." She made a sound that was half laugh, half snort. "I haven't really dated much, at least, nothing serious."

"That's hard to believe. You're an attractive woman." Did

he really just say that out loud? At least the darkness would cover the heat climbing his face.

"Well, I haven't. I've been focused on working, getting my degree and finding my dream job in a nice little town to settle down in." Her matter-of-fact tone faded at the end.

"What if it's a stalker, someone you worked with in West Virginia?"

"The other rangers were all married or female. I don't think it's a stalker."

"There are two men out there now. Two. This is no longer random."

She crossed her arms and shivered, and he regretted his sharp tone.

"I just need to know, why the secrecy?" While he took her at her word that she didn't know her attacker, there was something missing. A valuable puzzle piece. Maybe if he got in touch with the person she called earlier, he could get definitive answers.

She tucked her chin. "I'm sorry. I can't..."

Heath bit back a frustrated sigh.

He set the back of his head against the flat stone wall and attempted to think of anything other than the warm presence of the woman beside him. Other than Tinsley, he'd had a couple women in town make it clear they were available if he was interested. Nice, Christian women whom he knew all about. Knew where they lived and knew their history. *And* weren't hiding stuff from him. But they'd never tempted him to give it a chance. To test out the waters. One, it felt like a betrayal against Kara. Two, he had Piper's heart to consider, not just his own.

What was it about Laurel Bell that grabbed his attention?

At some point Laurel's head slipped onto his shoulder, and he rested his temple on her soft hair. He wasn't sure how long he'd dozed when he jolted awake. Laurel did, too, and he pressed a finger to his lips.

Heath cocked his head, listening. A dozen yards away, labored breathing and the distinctive sound of approaching steps spun his heartbeat into a tornado.

Someone was nearby.

He withdrew his weapon then pulled Laurel up, directing her back, ever so slowly, keeping himself between her and the opening. She could hide in the back chamber. Through the cave opening, ebony night flooded into their hiding spot. As his eyes adjusted to the dim light and their surroundings, he urged her to the backside of the cave, until she hovered about a foot from the narrow gap she'd disappeared into earlier.

"Keep moving," he whispered. "All the way in. Wait until I tell you to come out."

She slid between the two huge slabs and vanished. Lord willing, if something happened to him, she'd be safe in there until morning. Eli or another officer would find them. No adult man could fit through that.

The unmistakable sound of shoes scuffing against rocks and crunching leaves snagged his attention from the hidden chamber, and Heath whipped around to face one of their pursuers, now hovering at the mouth of the cave.

They'd been found.

SIX

Heath ignored the buzz of adrenaline in his ears and tried to aim as the man charged at him. He fired once, but the bullet clipped his attacker's left side and whooshed out the cave's opening. Heath growled and lunged sideways. It was the same man from the swamp. Had to be. Slightly smaller in stature than Heath, he was agile and strong and trained to fight. Add to that they were sparring in a tiny area, and this could get ugly.

Lord, help.

When they slammed into the wall, Heath's back hit first, the air in his lungs exploding out in a grunt. His elbow jarred so hard into the stone that his grip on the weapon weakened, sending it flying. He grabbed his attacker's shoulders then flipped and smashed him into the wall. The man howled then threw a punch. Heath faked right, releasing his adversary's shoulders, his gaze roving the ground. Where was his gun?

His opponent rolled away and jumped up beside Laurel's hiding space, grabbing at his left arm with his right. The bullet must've scraped his arm. Heath's gut twisted as the glint of a black gun shimmered beneath a slice of pale moonlight cutting through the cave.

He dived at the man, straight for his legs, as the weapon discharged. Heath tackled him, expecting to feel the sharp burn of a bullet or bullet shards, but instead only heard his opponent's high-pitched yowl. Had he been hit by bullet fragments?

Heath straddled the man, squelching his weak struggles. He wrapped his arms around the gunman's neck to cut off air. The goal wasn't to kill him—just incapacitate him long enough for them to get away before the second man arrived. No, they needed this man alive so they could find out who he was working for.

His forearms dug into the man's windpipe as the anger he kept bottled inside bubbled up. Anger about Kara's death. Anger about the criminals who were let off too easily by bought-and-paid-for judges. Anger that this perp was targeting Laurel, a caring woman who didn't deserve this. His opponent's frantic writhing ceased.

"Heath?"

Laurel. He released his hold and rose unsteadily to his feet, keeping an eye on the unconscious man. Every muscle in his body shook, wired with adrenaline and uncorked emotion. Dear Lord, had he killed him? The gunman lay unconscious on his side, limbs sprawled, as blood leaked from a wound on the side of his forehead. Shrapnel must've hit him. Relief washed over Heath as he watched his attacker's chest rise and fall at a consistent rate.

He would never be comfortable taking another man's life, even in this extreme situation.

A fiery dart of pain radiated from Heath's lower leg, like a wasp sting. He peered down, twisting to see the back of his calf. Even in the dark, a small crimson spot was visible. Must've gotten hit by shrapnel, too.

"Are you okay?" Laurel's question broke through his haze.

"I am. Will be, at least." He couldn't see her well in the dark. She must be speaking through the narrow opening.

"He shot at me, and when a bullet hits a hard surface like stone, it breaks into a bunch of pieces. What about you? Are *you* okay?"

"I'm fine," she called from the chamber. "Should you…do you have anything to tie him up with? Handcuffs?"

"Not with me." He examined the area. His extra handcuffs were in his truck. He was wearing an undershirt beneath his T-shirt. That could work.

"What are you doing?" Laurel asked as he tugged his shirt off, then his white tank top. After shrugging his shirt back on, he found a sharp stone on the ground and stabbed it through the material until it created a hole. Then he ripped hard, shredding it into one longer piece of material. "Wait, did you get shot?"

"Just a nick on the back of my leg. My side is stinging a bit, but I'm good."

He hunched down, pulling the unconscious man's arms together behind his back. The forehead wound looked gruesome, but there was nothing he could do for him now.

Heath wrapped the strips of white material tightly around his attacker's wrists, snug enough it would take a lot of work to cut through it. Then he grabbed a few stones on the ground, including the sharp one he used to shred his shirt, and tossed them out the door.

"Is it safe to come out?"

Laurel sounded close. He turned to find her standing in the front chamber. She gaped at the perp then back up at him.

"I don't have handcuffs," he explained. "I can't tie him up with my shoelaces because I kind of need them on my shoes."

"Is he unconscious?"

"For now." Heath's skin felt clammy as the sweat cooled on his limbs, face and neck. He checked the ground, locating his gun lodged in a crevice near the hidden chamber, then checked the prostrate man's pockets. A knife, an extra cartridge for his weapon, and a high-tech walkie-talkie device. No phone. "We need to move. He could wake up soon." He tossed the items through the cave's mouth.

They might end up spending the night in the forest. It wouldn't be summer vacation camping mode, but he'd make sure they survived. No matter what, she couldn't stay at her cabin alone. Couldn't *be* alone. He currently had no way to contact Eli or Chief Lane. If Eli tracked his phone, they'd likely send officers out in the woods near his truck. But that could take a while, especially in the dark.

They climbed out of the cave, and he scouted for unwanted company. So far, nothing. He led her down the path and to the right up a steep set of natural stone stairs that ended up above the cave.

"We need to climb up here to get to the trails uphill. Grab the handrails. These can be slippery."

"Do you think the other guy left?" she asked as they scaled the stairs leading them toward the visitor parking lot.

"Hard to tell. Could be they split up…and lost each other." They reached the top, and he scanned the area. "I don't see anyone. Let's move."

Several minutes later they reached the wooden stairwell connecting the trail to the parking lot. He paused halfway up it to let them catch their breath.

"I am exhausted," she panted.

"Are you saying you'd rate night hiking with a side of fistfighting a zero out of ten for family-friendly activities?"

She snorted. "I'll give it at least a two out of ten because of the brave tour guide."

"I do what I can." Their gazes snagged, and his chest compressed.

She broke the moment by looking away. "Does your daughter like hiking?"

"Piper prefers swimming right now. Especially because Tucker's girlfriend, Sarah, is a former Olympic swimmer. She'll be coaching at the local Y this summer, and Piper wants to be on the swim team." He motioned. "Ready to move?"

"You might need to drag me. Where are we going?"

"Once we cross the parking lot, we'll take the main road to Rimrock down. Your cabin is across Highway 126, maybe a half mile. There's a landline, correct?"

"Yes, but..." She frowned. "You want to hike to my cabin?"

"Not really. But we don't have a choice. With another armed man roaming the forest in between us and my truck, that's risky. I need to call Eli. Get officers up here to arrest that perp ASAP, and the closest phone is the cabin." He glanced behind them.

Heath led them through the empty parking lot. He'd never been up here at nighttime, because Rimrock closed at dusk and was only open from May to October. It felt eerie jogging across the empty parking lot, the plain brown bathroom structure staring at them, the two doors like huge eyes. An owl hooted in the distance, and the wind rushed past with a soft wail that lifted the hair on the back of his neck.

Half an hour later they spilled out onto Highway 126. Heath paused. Only cricket choruses and the distant rumble of thunder sounded.

"Your cabin is down this way." He pointed ahead of them. "We have two choices—stay on the road and take the driveway to it, which is an easier walk but more dangerous because we're in sight of any vehicle driving by. Might take us thirty minutes or so. Or, we head straight into the woods here and down this hill. It'll take longer, but we'll have cover in the trees, and we can approach the cabin from the upper ridge to make sure it's clear before entering." He turned to her. "What do you think?"

"I'd rather take the safer route, through the forest."

"Good. My thoughts as well. This part is downhill, but we have to climb back up in a few hundred yards."

She squared her shoulders then yawned. "Let's do it."

He chuckled. "You're a tough cookie, Laurel Bell." He patted her elbow, the gesture purely out of respect for her endurance and positive attitude. But she froze, her features stiffening so it looked like she would cry.

"I'm sorry." He withdrew his hand. What had he said? "I was teasing. I shouldn't—"

"It's all right." Her chest shuddered. "My dad used to call me his little cookie. I guess…when I was really young, my mom made her family's famous chocolate chip cookies, and I wasn't to be trusted around them."

"You could put some cookies away, huh?" He started down the steep embankment beside the road, motioning her to follow. Was her dad not alive anymore?

"Dad said I finished off half a dozen in one sitting."

The sound of a car's engine stopped them both short.

"Move!" Heath clasped her hand and pitched forward, low to the ground. They were about fifteen feet down the embankment, partially hidden from the road. Still, it wasn't a pitch-black night. The moon perched half-full in the sky, and the car's brights were on. He urged her to stay close as they slid on their backsides through the dirt and weeds to the bottom of the embankment where the tree line started.

Laurel matched his frantic pace, shaking and bumping into him as the car neared. It sounded like a smaller vehicle, and the engine revved as it climbed the ascending highway. Someone was in a hurry. He prayed the driver hadn't seen them cross the road. Laurel was a trouper, but neither of them had much gas left in their tank. Exhaustion was taking over, and they wouldn't be able to run away this time.

Laurel's limbs quivered as the car roared past. They weren't that far from the woods, but it still felt like they were lying in the open like a mouse in a field with a hawk circling overhead. She pressed into Heath, their arms jostling because he still held her hand.

They crab-crawled down the embankment, then he let go of her. Snarled bushes lined the edge of the woods like a natural fence. Heath pushed through first then aided Laurel.

"Watch out, they're sharp." He steered her between the brambles, then the cool air of the forest enveloped them. The trees were spaced farther apart in this area, and the moonlight followed them like a spotlight.

Her shoe hit a pile of sludgy mud, and she pitched back. He secured her arm, holding her upright, his concerned gaze boring into hers for a searing second. Searching. Desperate. No doubt wondering what she'd been holding back from him and why these men weren't giving up the chase. Then he surged ahead, but not before she noted disappointment in his eyes.

With each stride, her body withered under the weight of her secrets. Under the knowledge that he could've been shot back in the cave, because of her. Could've been killed. Not telling him who she was and what happened to her—it was for his own good. Protection to keep him and Piper safe.

His daughter couldn't lose her father, too. Not like Laurel had all those years ago.

"I'm pretty sure the man in the cave was the same man at the swamp." He huffed as they continued toward her cabin. "What I don't know is who the second man was with him. No idea if he got lost and turned around, then went back to the car." Heath slowed, and she raised her arms to keep from crashing into him. He turned, facing her. "I also don't know what you were doing in a California hospital as a child when your paperwork said you're from West Virginia."

Just lie, a voice screamed from within as she brushed past him and continued through the small valley. She'd been doing it most of her life, after all. Lying. *It's for their protection*, Tim had reminded her when she called him last year, struggling with the half-truths and outright lies she'd told a new friend. *And yours. You don't know who you can trust, Laurel.*

Right now, she was one hundred percent confident she could trust Heath Calhoun. More certain than just about anything else in her life. And for some reason, it felt important and necessary to tell Heath who she really was.

But his family... Piper. She winced, not meeting his eyes.

Heath released a heavy sigh, then resumed hiking. Exhaustion made her head spin, and her legs felt like they weighed a hundred pounds each. Branches slapped them and twigs fractured beneath their shoes as they made their way toward her cabin. She lagged behind, going through the physical motions as her mind clouded over.

Heath was involved. Completely immersed, whether she liked it or not.

The brain fog cleared, and her frame wilted. He deserved to know. Deserved to understand why she'd kept details from him. As they pushed through the trees and began an ascent toward the hill overlooking her rental cabin, words slipped out that felt like an apology and a confession.

"I…was involved in a crime when I was a child. And because of that, I've had to hide who I really am."

Heath did an about-face, and even the faded moonlight couldn't hide his thoughtful frown. "You're in WITSEC."

"I am. Have been, most of my life. I'm sorry I hid that from you. I was told to contact my handler and not share anything with law enforcement until I did."

"So, you are from California."

"Yes. Though I lived in West Virginia since high school."

"Your handler, that's the person you asked to call earlier—at the station."

She chewed her lip, her worry about not reaching Tim peaking again. "Right. His name is Tim Polling. He works at the San Francisco US Marshals' office. He didn't answer, and the last time I checked the phone in your truck, he hadn't called back. It's not..." Her whispered words spun away in the wind.

"Not what?"

"It's not normal. He always picks up, and the couple of times he's missed my call he calls back within an hour or two."

"Have you spoken to him recently, before your attack?"

"Yes, I spoke to him about a week ago, right after I moved here." She blinked away tears. "He called to make sure I was settling in."

"Thank you for telling me. It's imperative that we reach him."

"I know. I'm sorry for withholding that information—I was just trying to do what he told me to. Trying to...protect you and Piper and Molly."

"I get it." His gravelly voice touched her with its grace and understanding.

They set off again, clambering the rest of the way up the hill, the reality of her dire situation a heavy weight between them.

A while later, he motioned to slow down. "We're almost to the top."

As they reached the peak, Heath crouched beside a cluster

of trees circling a boulder. Laurel joined him, crashing to the ground in a boneless heap.

"We're not far." He pointed downhill, and she peered past him. The three-room cabin she rented sat in a cleared field, surrounded by about an acre of yard. Their location on the ridge afforded them a view from about two hundred yards away. A little red shed out back confirmed this was the right place. Her first few nights here had been peaceful. Uneventful, other than an owl hooting nearby early one morning and the choral croaking of frogs after an evening storm.

But that sense of safety had been ripped away from her at the swamp. Now she just saw an isolated structure with copious hiding places for assailants. She shuddered. "I can't imagine being here alone now."

He narrowed his eyes, his head dropping. "Wait a minute, that's not your car there, halfway up the driveway?"

"Where?" Laurel leaned forward to see around the foliage, her right shoulder pressing into Heath's left arm. She almost fell into him when she realized a dark blue, older model SUV sat in her driveway. Her Subaru had been towed to the police station so the men could inspect it for prints and damage.

"No, isn't mine at the station?"

"Sure is." Heath's tone was sharper than a knife. "That's the vehicle that shot at us after my tire deflated." He glanced at her. "Does any of this mirror what happened to you when you were younger? The crime…you were involved in?"

She sat back on her heels and rubbed her hands over her face. Weariness evaporated her cautiousness about sharing everything. "It's hard to say for certain. The man…who committed the crime against my family is behind bars for life."

"Are you sure of that?"

"Tim said so the last time we spoke. But I can't be absolutely certain until I talk to him."

"Understood."

She found a little mossy stump, swiped a few leaves and twigs off the top and sank onto it. Her whole body ached, her head throbbed, and her throat still burned from screaming that morning at the swamp. "I guess I'm not getting the rest that the doctor ordered tonight."

He took a knee next to her, and his intense perusal sent a current of warmth up her neck and into her cheeks.

"Not at the moment, no. Soon." He returned his observant gaze to the cabin, a lit-up dot through the foliage. "Did you leave a light on?"

"No, but there's a motion-sensor light on the front porch and one inside, in the hallway."

A faint, male voice carried up to them. Heath gestured for quiet, then he peeked out, head cocked.

"Looks like the lights came on because you have company," he whispered. "I only see one man. Let's sit tight, keep watch. Once he leaves, I'm going to try and get inside to call out."

"I can't believe Tim hasn't tried calling me, especially if—"

She clamped her mouth shut. She'd almost said August's name. But Heath couldn't know about him. Besides, August was still behind bars. Maybe the criminal in another case her dad had solved many years ago had been released and was coming after her.

The sound of a car engine grabbed their attention. Through the shadowed landscape and the trees, Laurel made out a man jogging from her cabin to the blue SUV.

Then he jumped into the SUV and did a three-point turn at a fast rate of speed, kicking up the gravel and spinning the tires as he peeled away. When he was halfway up the winding driveway, she realized the driveway curved toward their hiding spot on the ridge, and if it were broad daylight, he would see them. Heath must've had the same thought, because he set his palm on her shoulder and pushed her lower, to the ground.

Suddenly a red flash lit up the night, then an explosion in her peripheral vision sent her and Heath stumbling back. Flames engulfed the cabin, a giant inferno that made her chest feel like it was caught in a vise grip.

"No!" Tears flooded her face as she reared upright, and her ears rang from the sound of the crackling, sizzling fire down the ridge. Her dad's things, most of the memories from her childhood, lay in the wood structure. *Gone. All gone.*

"Laurel, get down." Heath tugged at her arm, urging her back to the ground with him. "The driver will see us."

But it was too late. The SUV had slowed halfway up the driveway, and a slammed door evidenced that the man must've seen her frantic movements through the trees and gotten out to investigate.

"Hey!" A shout rang out.

"We have to run!" Heath clasped her wrist and dragged her to their right, away from the driveway.

The car door slammed again, and the driver hurtled through the forest. Toward them.

A prayer fell from her mouth as they fled. "God, help us."

SEVEN

Every muscle in Heath's body longed to let loose and sprint, just go all out, but he couldn't for two reasons. One, Laurel was dragging, and he didn't blame her. She'd had a traumatic, exhausting day. And two, it was nearly impossible to run full speed through the rolling, woodsy terrain. He hitched his stride slower, relying on his memory and internal compass to get them as far as he could from the armed man who'd lit her cabin on fire.

"Where…are we going?" Laurel huffed as they scooted down the ridge, closer to the burning cabin.

"Straight ahead, but bypassing the cabin. The Allegheny River is a third of a mile past it. The current is pretty strong this time of year. We'll jump in and get away quickly."

Laurel moaned, and a burst of sympathy blew through him. Talk about tough. She'd dealt with more stress than most in a twenty-four-hour period and hadn't surrendered, and his respect for her was sky-high. He glanced up, where stars dotted the vast expanse, his mind dialing back to Laurel's simple, pleading prayer. *God, help us.*

He added his own silently as they jogged. *God, please help us get away from this man.*

Heath had struggled with his faith after Kara's death. Logically he knew it wasn't God's fault. He knew they lived in a broken, sin-riddled world. People passed away. Tragic accidents happened. Human bodies failed. But after losing his mom in an accident as a young man, then Kara's passing, his faith had been shot up like a target at a gun range.

Too much, he'd cried out to God. *It's too much for me, Lord.*

It was only his dad's stalwart belief in God and perseverance in living for Christ after Mom died that helped Heath realize he would dishonor his wife's life and her faith in God if he turned from the One she loved most and now spent eternity with.

But it had been, and still was, a struggle to find his way back to peace in his relationship with Jesus.

Heath guided Laurel around a cluster of trees and through an open field surrounding the cabin. She let out a coughing gasp as the heat from the fire blew over them, the smoke assaulting his nose as they sprinted through the trees at the edge of the yard. He prayed the embers wouldn't catch on any dry branches and start a forest fire.

Heath urged Laurel on. They were so close. He was pretty sure he and Kara had kayaked past this exact spot, taking a leisurely ride downriver along the edge of Holloway.

The nick of shrapnel from the cave prickled his calf as he jogged, but he ignored it. Why was Kara on his mind so much tonight?

Because, he admitted to himself, he'd been feeling guilty all evening. He couldn't deny that Laurel had captured his attention. Not just her dangerous situation, but her wholesome physical beauty and the depths he glimpsed when she dropped her mask. She was an intelligent and thoughtful woman, no doubt, and her struggles both about her past and about the terrible day she'd had instilled in him a high level of respect for her tenaciousness.

"How much farther…to the river?" she panted.

"Not far." His quads cried out as they stumbled downhill. He put on the brakes, jamming his shoes into the earth, so they didn't tumble headfirst on the sharply inclined ground. Branches thwacked them in the face and loose stones raced them downhill as they reached the bottom and the riverbank.

The ground rose slightly then curved lower, the last embankment before the water. A small inlet sat between them and the river, and Heath leaped in, then turned to reach his hand out.

Water droplets splashed his face and neck, and he wiped them away. "Almost there."

She followed him, and he caught her, holding her upright as water sprayed them. It was colder than he expected for late spring, made worse by the cooler night air. The slivered moon shone above, directing shafts of moonlight that dotted the miniature whitecaps rushing past in a tempo that sent goose bumps along Heath's limbs. All the rain they'd received this spring had caused the river levels to rise.

"I'm not the best swimmer," Laurel admitted in a shaky voice.

"I've got you." He locked his left arm with her right one. "The Allegheny River and I are old friends. Just call me Heath 'the raft' Calhoun."

She smiled briefly, shaking her head, and he swallowed his concern about the rushing current. A shout carried down from the rise they'd just ascended, and Laurel whipped around. Their pursuer hadn't given up.

"Come on." He stepped all the way in, testing the depth. Soon it reached his thighs.

She took a step, too, but then stopped. "I'm scared."

"I'm right here." He urged her farther into the river like a pastor preparing for a baptism. "I've got you."

She hesitated, then to his surprise Laurel jumped into his outstretched arms. He embraced her, and the water swallowed them whole. Cold prickles covered his limbs, and the slurping swish of the river filled his ears. They were immediately caught by the vigorous current, bobbing along like human buoys. He kicked out, his boots scraping the bottom, and then tried to stand upright so Laurel could draw in a full breath. Her hair plastered to her face, and a quick glimpse of her expression sucker-punched him. She was terrified—but she'd done it. Jumped in. Because she'd trusted him.

The feeling was singularly amazing and humbling.

"Hang on to me." He pushed off and turned, one arm still anchoring her to his side. He'd swum a ton as a kid, in this river and the community pool. Water training was a part of his job he enjoyed. He was no Olympic swimmer like Sarah, Tucker's girlfriend, but he could hold his own. Still, this situation was dangerous. Unpredictable.

Heath roped his arm firmly around her waist as the current played with them. He gulped air just as a wave splashed into his face. He inhaled water and his lungs froze up, desperate to cough it out. Using his free arm and his legs to propel them closer to the center of the river, he burst above the surface to spit it out and cough.

"Heath!" she cried.

"I'm here. Keep your face above…the surface. Yes, like that."

He attempted to gauge their position. The river stretched about thirty yards across in this section. Not very wide. They needed as much distance from their pursuer as possible.

A faint shout carried from upriver. Heath blinked away the water and shook his head. The gunman stood on the riverbank, water to his calves. Dark hair, goatee, young-looking. Definitely not the man Heath fought at the swamp and in the cave. His vision blurred from the repeated splatters of water pummeling his face. *Who was he?*

Laurel circled around, her hip bumping his as she tried to look back and flutter her arms. She raised one hand above the surface. "He has a gun!"

"Hold your breath," Heath shouted then plunged below the surface. They remained submerged a few inches deep when a series of whining sounds careened across the surface.

Bullets. *God, please get us away from him.*

Just when his lungs began screaming, Heath scissor-kicked them up, breaking the surface. He gasped and dragged in oxygen, then kicked forcefully to get them farther downstream.

The river tossed them to and fro like an angry liquid monster he had no way to fight. Instead, he concentrated on keeping Laurel in his arms and his face above the surface. When he glanced back, the bank where the gunman had been standing was empty.

Would the man follow them?

"We lost him," he shouted over the rushing current.

She didn't answer, and it hit him like a blow that Laurel had gone limp. He adjusted his hold, pulling her close and kicking so he could lift himself higher in the water and see her face.

Dark hair slicked back. Pale skin and closed eyelids.

Oh no. He couldn't tell if her chest was rising and falling.

God, help me save her.

Laurel hacked forcefully, struggling to sit upright. Her head pounded as she gagged on the water spewing from her mouth. Memories of the swamp flashed through her muddled mind. No, this wasn't the swamp. Where—

She was flipped over like a doll, to her side, and the rest of the water erupted from her in heaving coughs. Where were they? She wriggled her arms, trying to wipe the liquid from her face and mouth. Cool, damp sand rubbed against her palms and stuck under her fingernails.

"We're on an island." Heath's voice, low and steady. "We lost the gunman."

She closed her eyes and slumped onto her back on the gritty earth, overcome by exhaustion. He sounded as tired as she felt.

"Is your leg okay, from when you were shot at in the cave?"

He shook his head. "Don't even feel it."

She reopened her eyes, noting the slightly opaque color of the sky. The pitch-blackness was gone, which meant they were past the darkest hours of the night and dawn approached. "How did we…where…?"

"We floated downstream."

"I thought…" She swallowed, and her scratchy throat reminded her of the attack at the swamp. "I had a dream that we were on a boat."

"No boat. Just me. Remember, Heath 'the raft' Calhoun? You swallowed a lot of water again, and I had to get you out of the river."

She sat up on her elbows and looked around. Crickets chirped and the steady swish of moving water aggravated her frazzled nerves. All she could make out in the dark were trees and the river pulsing against the little shoreline. "And my cabin…was there a fire?"

"Yeah, I'm sorry, that part wasn't a dream." Heath rose and paced the immediate area then returned to sit beside her. "We're on a tiny alluvial island. I'm not sure which one, because I can't see how far we made it floating downstream. But it looks like it's a few acres, right in the middle of the river."

"Can the man find us?"

"Unless he has a boat, I don't think so."

She lay back down, gazing at the ebbing night sky. Stars

dotted the velvety heavens, beautiful and so, so far away. The same distance apart as the life she was forced to live and the one she'd always dreamed of.

"So, we're safe?"

He blew out a breath then lay beside her. "For now."

"I've been in WITSEC since I was nine and a half."

Heath angled his head on the rough ground until she could feel him watching her. "Sounds lonely."

"It is." She blinked as tears thickened her scratchy throat. "I used to dream of a normal life. My parents alive, a house with a big backyard, complete with an oak tree and a swing."

"You never had a swing or swing set?"

"No. My dad loved biking, so from an early age we went bike riding often. I was an only child, too, of older parents. I would've loved a sister or brother to swing with, play kickball or ride bikes with. You and Molly… I've only seen you together maybe an hour total, and I can feel the love bursting at the seams between you." She knew she sounded wistful, envious even, but she was too tired to care.

"I'm grateful for my family. I don't take my sisters and dad for granted."

"Well, I've only met Molly, and she seems great."

"She is." He cleared his throat. "I'm sorry you never had that. Siblings. I want that for Piper. Wanted it, at least." He paused, and the sound of the river's never-ending journey accompanied the rapid thumping of her pulse in her ears. "When I lost Kara, that dream was taken away."

"I'm sorry, Heath. It's so tragic." She hesitated. "Can you… would you remarry? Have more kids?" She chuckled softly. "The blonde nurse in the ER would be available if so."

"I'm not interested in Tinsley. Meeting someone new, someone who doesn't know my quirks and still loves me besides all that feels like too much work. And there's Piper to think about."

"I get that about Piper. Children get attached quickly." Their hands brushed in the sand. "So, what are these quirks exactly?"

"You know, I can't sit still. I move, wherever I am, whatever I'm doing. Even when I sleep, my feet move a bit. And I hate ice. In anything. A cooler full of ice? My downfall. I loathe the sound of it crashing together."

"Ice, huh?" She giggled, picturing the big strong man beside her running away from a blue cooler overflowing with ice. "Picnics must be a blast with you."

He shuddered. "The worst. Now let's hear about your quirks."

She pressed her lips together. "I would say my biggest issue is I can't sleep with any closet doors shut. Every door except the front and back doors have to be open."

"Aha. Make sure you can spot the boogeyman instead of him hiding from you."

"Exactly. Just like my dad taught me." Despite their treacherous situation and the bone-deep weariness in her limbs, she smiled up at the stars. "Promise not to tell anyone this?"

"Ooh boy, this should be good. Your secret is safe with me."

"I don't like coffee. At all." She stuck out her tongue and angled her face sideways to find him watching her, grinning. "I only drink tea. Black tea, green tea are my caffeine sources."

"No coffee? I may have to report you to the authorities. Pretty sure that's against the laws of adulthood." He yawned. "Man, right now what I'd give for a cup of coffee." A rumble originated in his chest, laughter and a moan. "Can we stop talking about it?"

How easy it felt with Heath, pretending all wasn't wrong in her life and that she wasn't alone and wouldn't have to leave Holloway and find a new place.

"I don't want to leave here." The words escaped before she could measure and weigh the danger of admitting them. "This town. I really like Holloway."

He didn't say anything for a couple moments, and then his arm brushed hers. "That's a WITSEC rule? That once your cover is blown you have to be relocated?"

"My dad brought down a half-century-old band of criminals. Their influence ran deep in San Francisco. There's every reason to believe they found me again, even if the main criminal who shot my dad is still locked up."

"Wait a minute." Heath sat up. "Was your dad a detective with the SFPD?"

Her chest constricted. She'd said too much, but there was no turning back. "My dad is—was—Rodney Campbell."

Even in the dim light, there was no mistaking the shock settling over Heath's features. "Rodney Campbell…who took out the Basile Brotherhood and was murdered by Leonard Basile's son?" He blinked. "You have… You're his daughter? The one who shot August Basile in the face?"

She clenched her eyes shut. "Yes."

"What's your real name?"

"Lauralee Campbell. But I've been Laurel Bell for so long, Lauralee doesn't sound right."

"I can't believe it. I remember the story. It was all over the news when I was young." When she opened her eyes, she found him watching her. "What do you prefer being called?"

Her throat tightened at his thoughtful inquiry. "I don't even care anymore, as long as *someone* calls me." A sob broke over her chest. "I've been alone so long."

The next thing she knew, Heath was sitting up and pulling

her toward him. One strong arm draped her back, pressing her into his side. She was wet and cold and scared, but she'd never felt so…so seen. So *not* alone.

"You're kind of stuck with me." His chest rumbled, and he tightened his hold on her. I was eleven when your dad was murdered, and I saw a picture of you on the news. I… I felt sorry for you. You were so small, all that dark hair and those big brown eyes. Not in a weird way, I just… I was still learning to pray, you know? Don't laugh, but I asked my mom to pray for you. I had this big happy family, a great home life. And you said your mom died when you were younger, right?"

"I was seven."

"Whew. Piper's age. Brutal. When I saw the news story, it piqued my interest, partly because of you and partly because didn't August come after you and your dad when you were in Redwoods National Park?"

She turned to ice in his arms. "Yes."

"I'm sorry, we can drop it."

"I'm glad you finally know, but that's kind of a selfish feeling."

"How so?"

"I don't want you or Piper or Molly getting hurt because of me."

"I'll do everything in my power to keep you safe and keep my daughter and my family out of harm's way." Heath's strong embrace eased, just slightly, but she felt it. Mourned its disappearance. "We should probably move to a more hidden spot at the center of the island and get some rest."

She drooped. "You might have to carry me there."

"I can do that." He stood, drawing her upright with him, and she leaned into him as they struggled through the gritty soil and broke deeper into the trees. Her legs wobbled, and the blisters that had formed on her toes and heel chafed from the movement. A couple dozen steps later they were situated under a large beech tree. The ground was littered by leaves and riverine grass, the briny scents of water and mud coating the air. A rounded rock pressed up to the tree trunk, and Heath carefully situated Laurel in front of it.

"I want to check the perimeter of the island one more time. Be right back."

"Okay." She leaned against the rock then drew her legs to her chest as Heath jogged off into the darkness. Once she'd ventured into the woods early like this, before dawn, to catch the sunrise through the tree tops. It had been one of the most peaceful mornings of her life, and looking back now, a gift from God. But she'd been alone, as usual.

Just as she found herself now as Heath did a lap of the area. The lapping river and flickering stars ushered in an overwhelming urge to pray.

"God, thank You for getting us away from those men." Her voice cracked. "Please watch over Heath and his family." She couldn't stand the thought of anything happening to him, Piper or Molly. Or Eli. Laurel slid down until her head pressed to the rock and she was nearly flat on the earth, her hands clutched over her middle. She closed her eyes, trusting Heath and trusting God. A verse flitted through her mind, sparkling like a shooting star in her memory. The verse Analiese suggested she jot down in her journal during the dark days after Dad's death.

Therefore I take pleasure in infirmities, in reproaches, in necessities, in persecutions, in distresses for Christ's sake: for when I am weak, then am I strong.

Weak. She felt so weak. How could being weak allow Jesus to be strong? Because admittedly, she couldn't do this—life, any of this—on her own.

God, I'm so weak. I need You. I need Your strength.

Footsteps flung her eyes open.

"Hey, it's me." Heath sank down next to her. "All clear. Other than a mother raccoon and her babies on the hunt for crayfish and minnows, we're alone."

She worked up a smile then closed her eyes again. She might be weak, but she had Heath. For whatever reason, God had sent this man to her as protection, and she was positive that she wouldn't have made it this far without him.

Sleep called, and she inched closer to his comforting presence then finally curled onto her side, head on her bent arm. The momentary peace her prayer ushered in dissipated like fog beneath sunlight. She'd endangered Heath and his family by telling him everything. They might be temporarily safe, but they weren't out of harm's way. Not by a long shot. Some criminal—from the Basile Brotherhood?—had eluded capture and was after her. Bent on revenge for her dad's role in wreaking havoc on their ranks.

Laurel fell asleep with a frown on her face and frightening dreams in her mind.

EIGHT

Heath jarred awake to the sound of oars slapping water. He sat up, dazed, as sunlight blinded him. Was Laurel—

A timid feminine snore originated from right next to him, and he drew in a measured breath. By the grace of God, they'd made it through the rest of the night without being found. He was especially grateful Piper was with her grandparents at the moment.

What time was it? The sun sent slivers of light through the beech's limbs, highlighting Laurel's dark hair and small form. He stumbled upright, peering through the branches.

An older gentleman wearing a wide-brimmed hat and hefting a large tackle box sat in a banged-up green canoe pushed ashore. The man struggled a bit as he dragged the watercraft on land, and Heath fought the urge to help him. First, he had to make sure this person wasn't connected to Laurel's attackers. A decoy.

Heath jammed a hand through his messy hair. What an astonishing coincidence that Laurel Bell—formerly Lauralee Campbell, the brave, once-famous daughter of slain San Francisco Police detective Rodney Campbell—had ended up in Holloway. Pennsylvania was practically another world compared to California.

No wonder she'd been so evasive about his questions.

The older fisherman tugged and pulled the canoe far enough ashore that eager river waves wouldn't snatch it back. Then he ambled across the dirt and sank onto a stone he must've known would be there, because he sat on it like he would a recliner in his living room.

Wait a minute…

"Carl Danson?"

Carl jerked his head toward Heath's voice, startlement on his sun-lined, bearded face. "Who's there?"

Heath climbed out from the thick brush. "Heath Calhoun, sir." He started forward, one hand out. "Boy, am I glad to see you here this morning. And your canoe."

"Mercy, Heath, I wasn't expecting you, let alone any other human beings. Although I did wonder where you'd got to, since Lawrence Wicker contacted me, said he heard you were on the run near the dam with armed men after you." The older man whistled then cocked his head. "That true? What kind of days are we living in? Hey, lookie there. Is that the woman the police are searching for?" He pointed behind Heath, where Laurel stood, her hair rumpled and eyes wide.

"He's safe," Heath called out, and Laurel carefully climbed through the bushes and approached them.

"Why, you are the one Lawrence mentioned. A young lady with dark hair. Mr. Buchanan was on the lookout. He's police, too, am I right?"

"Eli is FBI. But he's been apprised of the case and we're working together. Listen, do you have your cell phone?"

"I do, that dratted contraption." Carl pointed at his canoe. "Marjorie makes me bring it along. It's in there. See, in the plastic bag? You're welcome to use it. Code's 1-2-3-4. Kind of a dumb code, I understand, but who would want an old man's phone? Plus, that way I can't forget it." Carl guffawed, and Heath turned to find a hesitant smile lighting up Laurel's face.

"Think I can get a signal out here?"

Carl pushed his mouth out. "Now, that depends on the weather. Sunny and clear, you might could get reception. Stormy and cloudy, well then, I'm plumb foolish for being out here and I deserve the drenching."

Heath grinned. "Mind if I use your phone?"

"Have at it." Carl made his arm into an arrow that pointed to his canoe. "I owe you my and Marjorie's lives. Least I can do to say *thank you* is let you use my phone."

Heath rushed over, located the cell and unzipped the bag. He didn't want a reminder of what happened at the Danson's house. Shoving aside those dark memories, he checked the cell. Bars. *Thank You, Lord.* Then he keyed in Eli's number.

"Agent Buchanan here."

Heath's muscles loosened at the familiar voice. "I'd like to call for an Uber. I need a pickup beside the Allegheny River, near the overpass at Burnham Road."

"Heath, where have you two been?"

"All over, really. Rimrock, then we spent the night hiding out on one of the islands on the Allegheny. I just ran into Carl Danson. This is his cell. First thing, one of the men who came after us is at Rimrock. In the cave, wounded. I hope he's still there." His jaw ticked. "Unless the other man found him and got him out."

"I'll let Chief Lane know, see if he can send two officers out there ASAP. I found your truck and saw tire tracks near it, but there weren't any other vehicles nearby. Got your cell from under your truck. We searched the immediate area but called it off at midnight."

Heath cupped his hand over his cheek and the cell. "Listen, Laurel is WITSEC. Keep it under wraps for now."

"Really. Is she okay?"

"She's exhausted. Upset. But thank the Lord, we're both

unharmed. We need to reach her handler. His name is Tim Polling, San Francisco US Marshals' office."

"Got it. You know about her cabin?"

"Yes. We watched it go up in flames."

"You saw it? The closest neighbor called the fire department at 1:00 a.m., and Clay got in touch with me after they went through the remains." Eli paused on the double meaning of the word. "I'm sorry to say, so far he hasn't recovered much. The place is torched."

"We figured." Heath turned to keep an eye on Laurel as she spoke to Carl. "Everyone okay in Holloway?"

"All good." Eli's phone crackled. "I ended up staying at your dad's place to keep Molly and him company. She was a mess."

"I'm sorry, man. We had no choice but to run. They busted my front tire. At least three nails."

"I saw that last night."

They finished the conversation, agreed on a spot to meet in twenty minutes on Route 62, then Heath turned to Carl. "Thanks for the phone. I've got good news and bad news."

"Start with the bad." The older man didn't miss a beat.

"You won't be eating fish tonight."

Carl harrumphed. "And the good news?"

"I'm going to row you back to shore so you don't have to row yourself."

"Young man, that's the only exercise I get nowadays. Marjorie says I'm getting flappy wings." He lifted an arm and batted at the small amount of slack skin underneath. Carl dropped his arm and winked at Laurel.

Ten minutes later they scrambled up the shore, thanked Carl and trotted across the public-access parking lot. Heath's muscles were as taut as the rope Carl kept on the canoe, his brain buzzing with the sounds of a car approaching on the road and a lawn mower engine growling at a house downriver.

Laurel had been reserved since they loaded onto the canoe, and she glanced at him as they trod back onshore. "I have no idea what I said last night. I think I was out of my mind exhausted."

"Other than your Social Security number, bank account info and deepest fears, not much."

She elbowed him. "Yeah, right. Hey, what did Mr. Danson mean back there, that he owed you his life?"

"It's nothing," Heath ground his jaw, hoping she'd let it go.

She wiped her palms down her leggings. "I keep wondering if this is connected to August, even though he's in prison."

"I believe your WITSEC handler would've notified you immediately if he were released. You checked the cell I gave you for messages, right?"

"Yes, right before the tire went flat. There were no messages or calls from Tim." Distress coated her words.

"Eli has his info. He'll call him. If he can't reach him, we need to contact his Director."

Eli's SUV pulled in just as they broke away from the parking lot area. He drew up next to them, and Heath offered the front seat to Laurel.

She shook her head and climbed in the back, and Heath fell into the front, sprawling against the cushy interior. "You don't know how comfortable your basic car seat is until you've run a few miles through the forest, sat on rocks for hours and slept on the ground with raccoons and beetles."

"It was almost worth the view of the stars, though," Laurel mused quietly behind him.

"Almost," Heath replied, recognizing instantly the soft undertone of her voice. Gratitude, weariness and a hint of amazement that they'd survived the night's events mostly unscathed.

Eli glanced his way, brows arched, and Heath sent him a warning glare. Eli responded with a cocky smile, and Heath fought the urge to punch his arm. He ran a hand down his face instead. Eli was almost as bad as Molly.

There was nothing between him and Laurel other than mutual respect and admiration. Camaraderie. That was it. His jaw flexed. Yes, she was attractive and had depths that piqued his curiosity, but that was it. *Had* to be it.

Even if you wanted to go there, she isn't staying in Holloway. Her life, all the danger she's dealing with, can't connect to yours and Piper's.

A thought struck. It was imperative Laurel reach her WITSEC handler.

"Can I use your work phone? Laurel needs to call someone."

Eli grunted agreement then handed Laurel the phone, thankfully without any snarky comments accompanying it. Heath spun as she touched the numbers then set the phone to her ear. Several seconds later, her face fell.

"It went to his voicemail again." She handed the cell back to Eli after leaving a brief message.

"Same for me," Eli noted. "I've been made aware of your position in the WITSEC program, and I called the US Marshals' office. The call to agent Polling went to voicemail. I left a detailed message but haven't heard back."

Heath scowled at the trees flashing by as they headed into town. Where was Tim Polling? She needed someone smart and dependable in the US Marshals, and unfortunately it didn't sound like her handler was that. Who else could she rely on?

"Tim's message mentioned his Director," Eli added. "We need to get him involved."

Twenty minutes later he and Laurel staggered into his house. Axel and Forge swarmed them, sniffing at the forest and river scents on their clothes, the dogs' tails whacking their legs.

"The German shepherd is Axel, and this is Forge," Heath introduced the short-coated brindle canine. "He's a Dutch shepherd. Forge worked with my buddy Dave over in Corry during his career as a K-9 officer, until Forge was wounded a couple years into his service. We were able to adopt him after that."

"What happened to him?" Laurel sank to her knees, stroking the dog's lithe frame and scratching his powerful neck.

"Dave used him to apprehend a suspect. Drugs," he explained. "When Forge got him down, the man pulled a gun. See the tip of his ear, how it's missing a chunk? Forge moved just in time, but the bullet grazed his ear. Tore it. The vet sewed it back up pretty good, but then he found some hearing damage as well. It's minimal, but enough that they had to retire him."

"He looks perfectly healthy to me. Don't you, handsome." Her nails found the dog's favorite spot—two inches above his tail on his lower back. Heath chuckled as Forge's muscular back legs quivered, a look of pure pleasure in his dark eyes.

"Now he's never going to leave you alone."

"That's fine with me." She continued her ministrations with an unguarded smile Heath couldn't look away from.

Eli entered through the front door, and Heath addressed him. "Laurel found Forge's favorite spot."

"Yeah, well, my favorite spot is beside my fiancée, so let's get this done so I can get back to Molly." Heath pulled a gagging face, but Eli ignored him. "We're trying to get the last coat of paint on the master bedroom before she moves in after the wedding." A contented expression wiped away the normally intense look on Eli's face. "The wedding is only days away."

"Are you nervous?" Laurel stood back up, and Forge parked himself beside her.

"Just that I'll lose the ring." Eli glanced at Heath. "It's their mom's wedding band. It's a family heirloom."

A look of sympathy crossed Laurel's face, and Heath turned, disconnecting from the potent emotions the conversation was dredging up. His and Molly's dad had been pleased and honored to offer Eli his deceased wife's band, and Heath and his other two sisters—Katie and Laney—felt the same. Laney lived in Columbus, so they only saw her and her family a couple times a year, but Katie lived nearby and frequently helped with Piper. Molly and Katie had been godsends after Kara's passing, aunts and surrogate moms for his hurting little girl. Speaking of…

Heath crossed the entryway to his kitchen to grab a drink from the fridge. "Piper's coming back tomorrow morning. I don't know if I have time to drive back over there." His eyes flickered at Laurel, and Eli nodded his understanding.

"Do you think she should stay in Hershey longer?" Eli asked as Heath offered them both a pop or bottled water. Laurel accepted a water with a nod of thanks.

"I don't know." Heath rubbed a palm down his face. While his daughter enjoyed her visits with Kara's parents and her cousins, she usually wanted to come home. Missed Axel and Forge. Missed her bed. Sometimes in the bleakest moments of life, Heath wondered if Piper held out hope that her mom was coming back. That she wasn't really gone, or with Jesus, as he reminded her gently from time to time.

As an adult, he knew better.

"I hate to bring her back right now, but I promised only two days this visit." He scratched the scruff on his neck. He'd gotten used to the beard over the last three months, but it felt rough and grimy now. "Plus, they only had a four-day weekend, and I just remembered she has a school project that needs to get finished ASAP. It's due Friday."

Laurel stepped deeper into his living room then sank onto his couch. Forge followed her, trailed by Axel. Both dogs circled like they expected treats to appear in her hands. Apparently, Laurel had a new fan club in the Calhoun canines.

"Molly and I can go get her," Eli offered. "We could head out this afternoon. I talked to Officer Venetta and Chief Lane. Venetta offered to patrol the area while you and Laurel are here. Extra set of eyes."

As if on cue, Laurel leaned on the back of the couch and yawned. They both needed to catch a couple hours of sleep, or they'd be no good later today to give statements and go over the investigation and what had occurred last night.

"Any news about the perp I tussled with at Rimrock?" Heath asked.

Eli peered down at his cell. "Nothing so far. There are two officers out there now. Chief Lane said they'd apprise me of the situation once they arrived at the cave. You mean the one at the top, with the graffiti inside?"

"Yes. The big one." Heath addressed Laurel. "There's a bathroom upstairs. Molly has clothes you can borrow in the guest bedroom closet."

"A shower would be absolute heaven. And a nap." She dug her fingers into Axel's thick coat as he bumped Forge out of the way to get scratches from their lovely visitor.

An hour later, after Eli left and Laurel cleaned up, Heath threw together a midmorning breakfast of scrambled eggs and blueberry waffles, which they ate in companionable silence before he took a turn cleaning up in his bathroom. It felt good to wash off the grime and change out of the gritty, stiff clothes from last night. When he checked upstairs, Forge lounged on the rug beside Laurel in the guest bedroom, the open window allowing a breeze through the house. Axel remained on guard on his dog bed in the living room.

He walked out of his room, Axel trailing behind, then checked his phone before sinking onto the couch. No calls. He adjusted his long frame then rested his head on the huge pillow Molly had made of Piper and her mom's faces when Piper was four. It used to bother him, seeing Kara's beautiful smiling face sitting there alone on the furniture as he walked past and life continued on without her. Now he had moments, snippets of time where he would smile back at Kara. Imagine her with Jesus, with her baby brother, Silas, who had died at a young age.

Holding their second, unborn baby.

His vision misted, and he swiped his eye. He knew she was okay. Better than okay. Knew she loved him. Still, what he wouldn't give to talk to her once more. Tell her he was sorry.

What if they'd adopted, like she wanted? Would she still be here?

Don't let the guilt eat you alive, son. You can't change what God ordains, his dad had admonished him. *Good or bad. Life or death. When we trust in Jesus, we're gifted eternity, but yours hasn't started yet. Kara's started earlier than we wanted. You will see her again, but I know for sure she wouldn't want you living under a rock until yours begins, too.*

His dad's gentle warning drifted through his muddled mind, spoken a month after Kara's memorial service. Heath had been eaten up by sorrow and guilt, barely surviving each day. Barely noticing his grieving daughter. Too shocked and angry at himself to realize he still had a beautiful life and daughter around him that needed him.

His throat closed. Kara had been three months pregnant when her undiagnosed heart condition had worsened. That very day, she'd been fine when he kissed her goodbye and headed to the station as she and Piper sat at the table, Play-Doh containers tipped over on the top. Blue and green blobs of squishy shapes adorned the large white sheet Kara had laid over the table to corral the mess.

Then an hour later, he'd received the call. Their closest neighbor, Betsy Windover, reported that Piper was wandering the front yard. Heath's whole life had been upended when Betsy said the EMTs had taken Kara to the hospital via ambulance, and she had Piper, and would he like her to keep the sweet child the rest of the day?

For the thousandth time, Heath whispered a prayer to God and to his beautiful wife, who had died that day. "Forgive me, Lord. I'm sorry, baby. I miss you."

Laurel folded her hands together on her lap as she waited for Heath in his office at the station. A two-hour nap earlier had relieved some of the leftover brain fog and eased the physical exhaustion from the traumatic night in the woods, but much heart-heaviness remained.

Along with lots of questions.

Where was Tim? Why hadn't he returned their calls? And could August Basile have associates who'd been released from prison, and he'd sent them after her? It had been many years since she'd seen him, and back then she'd been a child, but she was certain the men she'd glimpsed at her cabin, in the cave, and before that, at the swamp, were not August Basile.

She would never forget those icy, pale blue, hate-filled eyes.

"I'm going to have you give your statement to Chief Lane, if that's all right?" Heath asked.

"Sure. Yeah." She stood abruptly, her pulse humming in her ears, then fell into step behind him as they left his office and hooked a right to another door two down from Heath's.

"While you're doing that, I need to go through some paperwork." He turned in the doorway. "Fill out forms. Clerical stuff. I'm going to reach out to Alex Vegas—Tim's supervisor. He must know something."

She nodded, clasping a lock of hair and twining it around her finger. Maybe Heath would get to the bottom of where Tim was and why he hadn't called her back. Because she couldn't deny that she'd begun to doubt Tim. Begun to wonder if…no. It couldn't be.

Could Tim be working with August and the Basile Brotherhood?

"It should only take about twenty minutes."

She nodded then turned, gazing at the sign above the door. *Chief Mark Lane.* A mustached middle-aged man rose as she slipped inside. Thinning black hair and warm, heavy-lidded eyes met hers. His slight build stood in opposition to Heath's taller frame. Once she made eye contact with Chief Lane, Laurel's troubled line of thoughts calmed. With all she had to hide in her life and her work behind the camera, plus the wide variety of people she'd been exposed to from a young age, she'd learned to read faces. Eyes. Expressions. Mannerisms.

It was one of the reasons she knew she could trust Heath. Wide and guileless, Heath's eyes told the truth, whether he realized it or not. And Chief Lane's eyes only held a steady warmth and resolve.

"Hello, Ms. Bell. Come in. See you in a bit, Sergeant."

Heath gave Laurel one more once-over. "You good?"

"Yes, thanks." She forced her gaze forward as the door shut behind her.

"So, Ms. Bell—"

"Please, call me Laurel."

"Laurel." He fingered the paperwork on his desk. "I do apologize that you've had such a difficult time since you moved to Holloway."

"It's been a little rough." What an understatement. She stared at a map of Allegheny National Forest on the wall over his head. "I hoped this would never happen to me. Especially here, in Holloway. It's so peaceful."

"Indeed." He cocked his head. "Because of this active investigation, Heath was required to disclose some details. I'm aware you're in WITSEC and that you have more to tell me about that. In typical Heath fashion, he also noted that it might be difficult for you to go into details about…what happened when you were younger."

She nodded slowly. Thoughtful Heath.

"Where would you like to begin?" he asked kindly but firmly.

On the wall, the clock ticked away. Moving forward, its minute and hour hands reminding her that time never paused. Never waited for the dead to catch up to the living. They were gone, and their time was…stopped. But her life was still ticking. She still had breath in her lungs. She wouldn't let these criminals steal anything else from her.

"My dad is Rodney Campbell. My original name, on my birth certificate from All Saints Hospital in San Francisco, is Lauralee Campbell."

"Huh." Chief Lane reached up to rub two fingers across his mustache. "It seems that bravery runs in your family."

She shook away the compliment. "I'm sorry I brought this sensationalized case to your little town."

Chief Lane stood and trod across the room, his gait uneven, as though a hip or knee bothered him. He approached the far wall and pointed to a picture of a petite, dark-haired, middle-aged woman and a slim young man, maybe in his early twenties, in full police uniform.

They both smiled proudly, their expressions resembling each other.

"This is me and my dear mother the day I graduated the police academy in Erie. She was killed by a drunk driver two days after this picture was taken. Two days." He stroked his mustache again. "I had no idea this would happen, and that working toward establishing a commission on ending drunk driving with the Commonwealth of Pennsylvania would become my mission in life as an officer as well as during my time as chief. You see, sometimes our mission in life comes from what happens to us."

Sometimes our mission in life comes from what happens to us. Her photography. The pictures of all the beauty in the world. Was that why she craved capturing God's creation, human and animal—in all its shapes, colors and forms—with her camera, because she'd seen and experienced such ugliness?

He hobbled to his desk and dropped into his chair. "Now, let's get your description of the events before Sergeant Calhoun comes back in here. He'd like to do a conference call with your handler's Director."

Forty-five minutes later, Laurel had given her statement, gone through another stack of mug shots provided by Chief Lane and tried calling Tim on the burner cell phone again.

She paced in Heath's office as he took a call at his desk, once again noting the strong contours of his features and how he took charge of every situation, but not in a bullying sort of way. Her stomach growled, still complaining after their lack of dinner last night and the strenuous hike.

Heath said goodbye and ended the call, then set his cell on the desk. "There's an APB out for the vehicle that shot at us." He spun the chair back and forth as he spoke. "No sign of the man in the cave, unfortunately. He must've woken up and made his way out. They did find blood samples, so those are being sent to the forensics lab in Erie."

Her heart tripped over. Had the man who burned her cabin down found the wounded assailant and picked him up after chasing them?

Speaking of. "Could I go out to the cabin and see if there's anything left?" Her chest ached as she considered the photo album her dad had made for her years ago, his police uniform and his badge that she'd kept. Were they all gone?

"I was going to meet one of the new rangers out there in an hour. Clay Reiger, the ranger who pulled up at the swamp? He transferred here from New York State after Tucker hired him on. He's a former Air Force firefighter and has extensive background in arson investigation and fire forensics. He's been working in…your cabin, to see if getting prints or cause of fire is possible."

"Can I come along?" She knew she sounded desperate, but she was anxious to see what—if anything—remained of her precious past and her dad's life.

"I think we can manage that." Heath halted his swiveling motion then grabbed a pack of white mints from his top drawer and popped a couple into his mouth. He offered her some, but she shook her head, and he tucked them back inside. "I'll let Clay know we're headed out soon. Eli and Molly are picking up Piper this afternoon and should be back by six. I don't know about you, but that nap wasn't long enough for me."

"Should I stay there—at your house?" Chief Lane had mentioned getting her a hotel room in town, but the thought of living in that sterile space by herself the next few days held no appeal. "I could stay at a hotel instead."

"Would you *rather* get a hotel room?" His brows knit together as he spoke, and his perceptive gaze took in her slight shudder.

"Not really. But I don't want to put you or your family in danger." She swallowed. "Because I'm starting to doubt…"

"Doubt what?"

"Maybe not doubt. Maybe *wonder* is the better word. Tim has always been on top of things with my case. With me." She stood on unsteady legs. "I don't believe he'd leave me hanging if something changed with August Basile's case."

"Speaking of that, I took a look at the file. August Basile is serving three life sentences for your dad's murder and for attempted murder and aggravated assault. There's no way he'd be paroled after twenty years. I have a call with the prison administrator. We'll see what I can find out."

He stretched in a thoroughly masculine way that was impossible to look away from. She forced her gaze to the floor.

"Thank you, Heath." She needed to keep her mind off things she had no right to think about. Heath Calhoun didn't want a woman in his life with baggage the size of a dump truck. "You've been a lifesaver. Truly."

"What flavor?" He stood, edged around the desk toward her.

She looked up at him, caught off guard once again by how his surprising changes of subject eased her tension. He referred to the candy. "White's my favorite. Pineapple."

"Now, see, I think cherry is the best."

"To each his own," she teased. "Cherry isn't too bad."

He stepped closer, their loose smiles straining as the air

crackled between them. A connection built on what they'd been through and the growing trust between them.

That was it.

Heath reached out, cupped her elbow. It was a brief touch, and the warmth from his hand circled her arm and spread through her chest. The urge to lean into him, to rest against his strength again like on the island, to let someone else take on the weight of her unpredictable world, almost drove her to do something irresponsible.

Like hug Heath.

He was an officer investigating the crime committed against her. Also, a guardian when the men came after her. That was it. He was still grieving his wife, while Laurel would likely have to leave Holloway. There was no sense in getting attached—even if he was incredibly easy to get attached to.

NINE

Heath steered his truck down the winding driveway leading to Laurel's rental cabin. Afternoon sunlight poured in through the windshield. Eli had called his dad Roger's tow truck in when he found Heath's truck with its flattened tire yesterday, and this morning Roger Buchanan replaced the damaged tire and checked the others. Because it appeared that no one broke into his truck or touched anything inside, Chief Lane had given Heath permission to drive it again. After Eli dropped Heath and Laurel off at Buchanan's Auto Body Shop at two, they had grabbed a quick bite on the way to meet Clay at the cabin.

Laurel's chicken salad wrap remained half-eaten in the fast-food bag, while he'd wolfed down his turkey burger in fewer bites than was good for his stomach. When she had offered him the other half of her chicken salad wrap, he'd thanked her but passed, rubbing his full stomach.

Once again her thoughtfulness reminded him of Kara. She and Laurel were dissimilar in appearance and in personality, but both women had shared food with him, and that earned bonus points in his book.

"Are you sure it's safe to bring your daughter back today?" Laurel's voice woke him from the walk down memory lane and a comparison he shouldn't be making.

"I don't know." He sighed. "I promised her it would be a short visit, and she'll be upset if I make her stay there. She also has a project to finish."

"Does she like visiting them?"

"She does, but we just celebrated Kara's birthday last week. It hits us both pretty hard and we get clingy to each other."

"I'm so sorry, Heath."

"Yeah, we miss her. I pray God will help me raise Piper right while still keeping Kara's memory alive."

"I have no doubt you're doing a wonderful job of that." She sipped her drink. "Do you get along with your in-laws?"

"I do. They're good people. Kara and I only dated a year before we married, but they welcomed me. She was an only child, and her parents longed to have grandchildren." He fought off a wave of melancholy. "Anyway, yes, they love having her visit." He pulled his truck in next to a black Jeep in front of the skeletal remains of the cabin.

"I can't believe it's gone." She let out a pinched breath as she surveyed the damage wreaked on the cabin by the fire last night. "If we hadn't seen it happen, I wouldn't believe it was the same place."

He cut the engine then met her troubled gaze. "I'm just grateful you weren't inside."

Her eyes widened, the bronze irises tracing his features as though measuring for sincerity, then she looked away quickly and grabbed the door handle. Laurel must've become a specialist in keeping people at bay and hiding her emotions, though he recognized why now.

They hopped out, and Heath circled the truck to meet her and walk together to where Clay stood outside.

Clay was average height, a few years older than Heath, and built lean like a runner. Tucker said Clay had participated in triathlons and long-distance races, and he looked like he could run circles around Heath. Clay held a small tool in his gloved hands.

"Heath. Ms. Bell." He pulled off a glove, tucked the tool under one arm and shook Heath's hand, then Laurel's. He addressed Laurel with a sympathetic expression. "I've done my initial readings of the place, and there's no doubt we're dealing with arson." He met Heath's eyes. "I found two flash points. Spots where the temperature burned hotter than anywhere else in the building. I'll have to send the rest of the reading to the lab in Erie. Now, about the arsonist. You spotted one suspect leaving here last night. Any idea what time?"

"Middle of the night. Midnight or 1:00 a.m., maybe?"

Clay led them closer to the structure, his voice and gestures animated. The man was passionate about his job. "See this mark here? This tells me the fire reached flashover, which is over a thousand degrees. That's common when there's a kitchen fire, but you weren't home or cooking, correct?"

"No, I hadn't cooked yesterday at all."

Clay's thick brows rose as his gaze bounced between Laurel and Heath. "Did you say the fire started then there was an explosion within a few seconds?"

"About that. It's hard to gauge exactly, but it was only seconds. Laurel, do you remember?"

"It happened so fast, I'm not sure. Maybe two or three seconds?"

"Okay. It sounds like an accelerant was likely used to incite the flames then."

"Which one?" Heath asked. "Gasoline?"

"I'm not sure yet." Clay ducked through the gray-and-black remains of the cabin's front porch. Heath followed, keeping Laurel close. Her breath hiccupped as she stepped into the ashy remains.

"Would you rather wait out here?" Heath asked.

"No. I need to see if any of my stuff is salvageable."

He seriously doubted that was the case, but if she wanted to do this, he'd be there for her. They made their way across what appeared to have been the main room. A piece of furniture resembling a couch sat in the middle; bits of upholstery and a small blue pillow remained, tucked beneath it like it had been hiding. If she'd been here alone…

"I'm going to finish my sweep of the kitchen." Clay trod cautiously through the mess to their left, where the hole that once housed a galley kitchen remained, marked by the blackened fridge and a length of melted Formica countertop.

"The table is gone," Laurel whispered. "And the pantry… looks like it was totally burned up."

"See this?" Clay knelt, pointing to a dark stain on a burned cabinet. "This is probably cooking oil or grease. If arsonists are trying to lay low, or cover their tracks, it's common to use grease instead of gasoline. They think it's smart, but if the fire starts when no one is home, it just comes across as a rookie mistake." Clay clicked his tongue.

"But the man must've known she wasn't here," Heath noted. "Why do all this?"

"Maybe it was part of the plan to chase her out of town? Or her attackers were determined to destroy evidence." Clay squinted at Laurel. "Is there anything in the bedroom they might've been after?"

"I doubt it. I don't have much. Just my clothes and personal items." Her voice hollowed out. "There were some special mementos…from my dad in there."

Heath's heart twisted. "Let's check it out."

They wove carefully to the back of the cabin. Gaping walls and a busted, heat-cracked window allowed a breeze through the structure. He and Laurel entered the small single bedroom. Across the hall, there appeared to be a bathroom, where a wood vanity had melted down to half its previous height, leaving the sink crooked and covered in black debris.

Laurel shifted through the bedroom like she was in a trance, investigating scraps of the bedspread and tiptoeing through piles of ash. Tiny sniffles accompanied every movement. The trauma of seeing all she owned gone up in smoke after the terrible day and night she had must be too much, and he almost grabbed her and guided her outside.

What had she done to deserve any of this?

Suddenly a sob tore from her mouth, and she fell to her knees beside the remnants of the bed frame.

He hurried over. "What is it?"

She knelt in front of a blackened photo album. The slot on the cover was empty.

"My dad's…picture. It's gone."

"Where, on the cover?"

"Yes." Her body shook. "There w-was a picture of me and dad with our b-bikes. Near the Golden Gate Bridge."

"You're sure it was in there when you moved here?" He gentled his voice and set a hand on her upper back. Heath longed to pull her into his arms and comfort her. "Is it possible it fell out in the moving process?"

Footsteps alerted him to Clay's presence. The fire ranger hovered in the doorway. "What's up?"

Heath pointed. "She says the picture in the album is missing. It was of her and her dad near the Golden Gate Bridge."

Clay edged closer, cautiously stepping over heaps of ash and the blackened bedspread. "Then I should bring that in for latent fingerprint recovery." He addressed Heath. "I'm not equipped to do that at the ranger station. You mind if I work on those at HPD?"

"Whatever you need," he answered, Laurel's shoulders shaking beneath his palm. "Can you give us a minute?"

"Of course. I'll go grab an evidence bag. Take your time."

Once he was gone, Heath sank down next to Laurel. She swiped at her damp cheeks, wearing a wounded expression as she contemplated the damaged album.

"You're positive the picture was still on the cover?"

"Yes. He had the album made for me for my ninth birthday. Right before he was killed." Her voice had steel in it. "I've never taken the picture out. I can flip through the rest and see if those are missing, too."

"No." He touched the top of her hand. "Clay needs to check for fingerprints. We don't want it to fall apart before getting those. C'mon, let's see if there's anything else you can salvage and bring with..." His words trailed off when she turned to look up at him, her features fierce.

"Where? Where will I take it? And what could've survived this inferno?" Her eyes welled up, overflowing, and he drew her upright then pulled her into an embrace as she cried, rocking in the circle of his arms. Heat broiled in his gut, as hot as the flames that had scorched this structure. Not only had the men torched her house and valuables, but they'd also taken one of her most prized possessions.

But why? To prove that was the reason they wanted her dead?

The closer they got to the killers after Laurel, the more he realized this had to be linked to her past. To August Basile. Heath pulled out his cell and texted Eli what they'd found.

Maybe Laurel's doubts about Tim Polling weren't unfounded. Could the US marshal have gone dark after betraying her?

Laurel clutched the clear bag holding the photo album from her dad as they drove away from the cabin, but her mind remained on Heath's hug. He had lifted her physically and emotionally with his presence. Her longing to have that in her life—a person to trust implicitly, to lean on—swelled painfully in her chest until her heart ached.

If only that strength remained when he'd let her go.

My grace is sufficient for thee: for my strength is made perfect in weakness. The Bible verse echoed through her mind.

How? How can I do this, God? She prayed silently as she stared out the window.

Clay had pulled on gloves then opened the pages carefully, because the plastic pages were scorched and brittle. From what they could see, every other photograph remained in the album except the cover.

Why had they taken the main picture? She shivered as Heath's truck AC blew over her. He clicked the vent down and adjusted it so it aimed at him.

"You think this is related to August Basile," he stated rather than asked.

"I don't know what to think anymore." Her voice sounded faraway, and weak. So weak. She had no strength left to fight this fight that felt as though it would follow her every day for the rest of her life.

My strength is made perfect in weakness.

"We're going to catch whoever is behind this and put them away for good."

She nodded, her tongue stuck to the roof of her mouth and doubts drowning her under a deluge of dread.

Twenty minutes later they pulled into the Holloway Police Department parking lot. Clay parked his Jeep next to them, and Heath rolled the window down.

"I'll get started on the prints." Clay's light blue eyes darted from Laurel's face to the album she held to her chest. Slowly, she released it to Heath, and he handed it through the window.

"I'll be as careful as possible," Clay promised.

She nodded, not trusting herself to speak.

"Thanks, Clay," Heath answered. "I'll be in there shortly."

The other ranger strode into the station, leaving her and Heath alone.

"Don't you need to go with him?" she asked.

Heath put the truck in Park then shut the engine off. Sunlight shone through the tinted windows, warming her cool skin. Would her life ever go back to normal? She shrank lower in the seat. Had it ever really *been* normal?

"I will. Right now, I want to stay with you." He eyed the parking lot, then grabbed the knob to recline his seat. It lay back and he rubbed a hand through his beard, scratching. "Think I should shave this?"

She huffed out a chuckle, taken aback by his random question. Heath was somehow professional but also down-to-earth, and he always seemed to know when she needed a distraction from her heavy thoughts and worries.

"I saw a picture of you without the beard on the fridge at your house. It ages you some, but not in a bad way." She plunged ahead. "I think you look nice either way. Right now, you just look more like a mountain man."

"Mountain man, huh?" He snickered. "Like Bigfoot?"

She shrugged, and the faintest smile tipped her mouth up.

"Piper and I play this game sometimes, where she hides, and I have to find her. I pretend I'm Bigfoot, make all these loud growling sounds and stomp around, then she runs away from me. But we only play it when I have the beard, because she says it's 'more like the real Bigfoot.'"

"Ha, sounds like fun. I'm sure she loves that." Excitement sparked inside her at the idea of meeting Heath's little girl. "When will Molly and Eli return with her?"

"A couple hours at least." He glanced at his cell. "Listen,

before we head back inside, I want to go over something else with you, and I didn't think doing it inside the station was a good idea."

Her muscles tensed. "What is it?"

"Will you tell me exactly what happened the day your dad was killed?"

She blinked at the passenger-side window, seeing the present but remembering the past she'd tried hard to forget. "After my dad busted the BB—the Basile Brotherhood—the city blew up with the news. He was heralded as a hero, but he just wanted to be left alone to work on the next case. Plus, he'd been shot and had to take off work for a couple weeks." Emotion stung her throat. "I loved having him home all that time. I made him play board games for hours, helped with lawn work just to be near him."

"I'm glad you have those good memories with him."

"Me, too." She tilted her head. "Dad was smart. He knew having his name splashed all over the TV didn't bode well. He knew..." She swallowed. "It must've been clear his life might be threatened at some point."

Heath traced the steering wheel. "The case was on the national news, too. Leonard Basile, August's dad, had funded the plan to assassinate Howard Brinks, the gubernatorial candidate a couple years prior." He shook his head. "Anyway, when I looked up the Basile Brotherhood, I learned they'd had a hold on that area of the city for years. Decades. What your dad did was smash the hornet's nest, but..."

"But what?"

"I think the past two day's events confirm that a few hornets got away."

Her chest rattled on her next breath. She couldn't deny what Heath said was probably true.

"I'm sorry for bringing all this up, I just wanted to get your perspective on the day your dad was killed."

"We were biking. His doctor didn't want him doing much else because of the bullet wound but said biking would be safe enough." She choked. *Safe.* Would she ever feel safe again? "There was a stretch of the trail with pretty easy access to a public parking lot. The officers who found Dad and me—and August—got there pretty fast. That's how they think August found us. He…" She closed her eyes. "He followed us that day, then waited in ambush. Kind of like what happened at the swamp."

"And he shot your dad."

She nodded. "Twice, once in the chest, once in his left arm. Dad fell off his bike, which crashed into me on my bike. We basically fell together, and in the chaos, my left hand ended up near his right leg and side. Dad…reminded me he had a gun, then he whispered to me before he passed."

"Do you remember what he said?" Heath's words throbbed with empathy.

"He told me to be brave." Tears threaded her words, and Heath reached out and placed his hand over hers. "I was so shocked, in pain, and it happened too fast to really think about anything. August was so intent on Dad I doubt he even noticed me. When I saw my dad's gun, I didn't think. Just acted. I sometimes wonder if I didn't care if August shot me, too. Dad was the most important person in the world to me, and my heart knew this wouldn't end well. That I would lose him, too."

"Laurel," he said in a soft, rough voice.

She forged ahead. "So I grabbed the gun, flipped the safety off like Dad taught me all those times, and fired. It was so loud I screamed, but I fired again. August fell backward. I couldn't even fathom that I hit him. I just stood and screamed.

I saw blood…and then two bikers came upon us. No, three. A family. The mom took the kid and screamed, too, made the kid turn around." She smiled slightly, but it was grim. "Sometimes in the darkest moments of the night I wish I'd gone over to him and actually killed him. That's terrible, isn't it? Wishing death on someone."

"It's not what God asks of us, no. But we are only human. August took your dad's life." His thumb stroked her hand. "Reports said you shot him in the face, and it struck his cheek."

"Yes. Disfigured him." She shivered at the memory of seeing him at the trial, his flat blue eyes locked on her. "The EMTs couldn't save my dad, but they saved August."

Heath grumbled under his breath, sharing in her hurt about life's casual injustices. "For what it's worth, I think you're brave, Laurel. Incredibly strong. You've been through a lot."

"I don't feel brave. I feel weak. So often it's like I don't have the strength to keep facing this. Keep living with worry and fear nipping at my heels."

"There's a Bible verse about that." Heath drummed his fingers lightly on the top of her hand. "C'mon, brain. Do your thing. Ah. Here we go. 'And he said unto me, My grace is sufficient for thee: for my strength is made perfect in weakness. Most gladly therefore will I rather glory in my infirmities, that the power of Christ may rest upon me.'"

Her breath swooshed out of her chest. "You know that one, too?"

"My dad's a pastor. I've had Bible verses jammed into me from the crib." But he grinned as though he welcomed that reality.

"The family that took me in after Dad died, the Heigels, were believers, and one time when I was struggling after my dad's death, Annaliese shared that verse. She suggested

I write it in my journal. I loved to scribble and draw, and I'd turn that verse into art."

"I'm glad you had them to guide you."

"Me, too." She angled her face toward him, and in the truck's interior it felt like they were the only two people on Earth. "You said something last night in the woods. Did you really follow my dad's case when it happened? You actually...prayed for me?"

A dull pink color flushed Heath's face, and Laurel took in his masculine embarrassment with veiled joy. The idea that he had thought about her when she was young and her life was upended, and he'd prayed for her—it felt like Christmas morning. Like a gift she'd never forget.

"I did. We had family devotions, and I brought you up often. I mean, it happened so far away. But there was something in your eyes that stuck with me. Maybe it was a God thing." He shrugged sheepishly. "You ready to go inside? Eli and I will be following up with Alex Vegas, Tim's Director."

Laurel nodded, and they headed inside. She was still stunned at what Heath had admitted about praying for her when she was little, and how it confirmed Annaliese's words from years ago.

God gives us each other so we can comfort and lift each other up. We aren't meant to live on our own, Laurel Grace Bell. Don't give away the blessing of others to do life all on your own.

A silent prayer fell from her lips as they walked inside. *Thank You, God, for giving me Heath Calhoun. Even just for a short time.*

Now, to keep her heart from getting too attached. Once this investigation was over—Lord willing, once these criminals were arrested—she would probably have to leave Holloway and start over again. And Heath couldn't be part of her new life. No matter how much she longed for that.

TEN

Laurel and Heath entered his house a few hours later, weariness dogging their steps. Heath held two boxes of pizza and a container of boneless wings, while she clutched a two-liter clear pop as well as the weight of the world on her shoulders.

When would this trial end? *Please, God.*

A little girl flew across the house, squealing. Forge and Axel trailed her, and Eli and Molly stood behind them, another child in between them. Eli's daughter? Despite her trepidation about meeting Heath's daughter, Laurel couldn't help smiling at Piper's clear-eyed exuberance as Molly came over and took the food and drink from Heath and Laurel, then she, Eli and the other little girl disappeared into the kitchen.

Piper was slender and lively, her hair the same color as her dad's, with wide, light brown eyes and a sprinkle of freckles on her nose and cheeks. After jumping into her dad's arms and receiving a growling, ticklish bear hug, Heath set her back down. Piper gazed frankly at Laurel with a curious expression.

"Piper, this is Miss Laurel. Laurel, this is my daughter, Piper." Laurel offered Piper her hand. "Miss Laurel is a nature photographer. She works with Mr. Tucker and Aunt Molly."

"Hi, Piper. I love your name."

The little girl pumped Laurel's hand up and down. "Thanks. My mom liked it, too. You have a camera?"

Laurel froze. Her damaged Nikon remained in the Holloway police station, and her backup camera had been burned beyond repair in the skeletal remains of her rental cabin.

"I do, but right now it's at your dad's station." She shoved back the dark trail of her thoughts. "I love taking pictures. You get to capture moments, animals and people and keep them forever." Her eyes misted. "Even when they're not with you."

"Yeah." Piper's single syllable turned into a full sentence. "I like that a lot. I like taking pictures, too."

"Maybe we can take pictures together and I can teach you how to work a camera."

"Yeah!" Piper hopped around like a bunny. Such enthusiasm.

"Hand slap or fist bump?" Laurel smiled, a genuine one as she flew back in time to those days when she and her dad would communicate about their days via the hand gesture. A slap meant a good day, a fist bump meant a hard day, but they'd made it through. Laurel's chest tightened. A hug meant a difficult day.

Oh, how she needed a hug from her dad right now.

Piper cocked her head at Laurel's hand then launched at Laurel instead, wrapping her thin arms around Laurel's middle. The tight, quick hug sent a jolt of warmth through her, and she barely had time to hug back before Piper let go and skipped away to the kitchen, where Molly had opened the pizza boxes and pulled out glasses.

Heath ambled over and joined her, their arms brushing as they took in the lively scene in the kitchen with Eli, Molly, and Eli's daughter Skylar, and now Piper.

"She's a bundle of enthusiasm," Laurel noted. "Ready to take on the world. Reminds me of myself two decades ago."

His countenance fell. "She gets that from her mom."

"I think she gets it from her mom *and* dad."

He shrugged, and they headed to the kitchen to eat with the rest of the group.

Two hours later Molly, Eli and Skylar pulled out of the driveway. Heath shut the door and locked it, then turned to face Laurel and Piper as they lay down another round of UNO cards.

"Piper, don't you have to take pictures of the moon?" Heath thumbed at the window. "For your science fair project?"

"Oh, man." The little girl considered Laurel, her eyes narrowed, lips mashed together in thought. "Can't Miss Laurel help me, so my pictures aren't blurry like the ones you take?"

"Hey, my pictures aren't that bad." Heath sent Laurel an is-that-okay look.

"Absolutely." Laurel stood and stretched, then turned and caught Heath watching her.

He averted his gaze, rubbing his palms down his jeans. "Piper, go get some socks on. And a jacket. It's still too chilly to walk outside barefoot." Piper whooped then darted up the stairs like the roadrunner.

Heath watched as Laurel padded toward him. "I have an older camera, not sure what kind. It's not as fancy as yours, but it's decent, and it works. It was Kara's, for her classroom."

"She was a teacher, right?"

"Elementary. Second and third grade."

Her heart faltered at the forlorn expression that ghosted his features before they returned to normal.

Piper tumbled back down the stairs as loud as a herd of elephants, then jumped up and down in front of her dad. A green-and-brown horse blanket cocooned her energetic frame. "Can we do the pictures on the deck?"

Heath's gaze swiped to Laurel, and she could read from his slanted brows and frown that he was calculating the safety of it.

"All right," he conceded, and Piper cheered. "We can go out and take pictures on the deck. But only for ten minutes. Laurel—" he addressed her "—I'll let the dogs out back to make sure…yeah. Then I'll check the doors and windows and go grab the camera. It should be in the guest room upstairs."

She nodded as he made his way around the downstairs living room, kitchen and entryway, fingering the window locks and doors before calling the dogs to the back door and releasing them into the large, fenced yard.

Then he mounted the stairwell, taking them two at a time.

Laurel turned to Piper. "What's your school project about?"

"It's for when the moon is different each week." Piper helped her round up the UNO cards then she took them from Laurel and shoved the pack in a drawer inside the ottoman. "When it's big and round, and when it's small and pointy."

One of the dogs let out an ear-splitting volley of barking, and Laurel pressed her fist to her chest.

"Forge, cut it out," Piper shouted, probably parroting her dad. "They like to bark at the raccoons and deer. They eat Aunt Molly's flowers."

But then the other dog barked, the volume escalating. Goose bumps crawled up Laurel's limbs. "Do they usually bark that loud?"

A masculine shout exploded from the second floor, then a smashing noise followed that sent Piper right into Laurel's arms. She pulled Piper close as the little girl whimpered, though it was barely audible over the commotion upstairs and the ferocious barking out back.

Another male cry, this one Heath's, carried downstairs like a crack of thunder. Laurel looked around and tried to calm her wild breathing. The men must've broken into a second-story window.

She moaned. The guest bedroom window. When she rested earlier, she'd left it open. Heath had gone into that room. *God, please keep him safe.*

"We need to hide," she whispered to Piper, her pulse drumming in her temples. The pantry. It was tucked into a corner of the kitchen, well hidden. What about Heath? Would he be okay? Where was his cell?

No time.

They scurried across the room, and Laurel directed Piper toward the pantry door. Her elbow bumped the kitchen counter, causing one of the pizza boxes to slide over the edge, where it crashed to the tile.

"Where do you think you're going?"

The alarmingly familiar male voice sent a shudder through her, and she pivoted, pushing Piper behind her as she faced the intruder who sounded like he'd reached the bottom of the staircase. "Get out of here!"

He slunk toward the kitchen, until his black-clad form came into view and her ribcage squeezed her thumping heart to a pulp.

"You got me dinner this time. Isn't that nice."

Black spots dotted Laurel's peripheral vision as he advanced on them, her swamp attacker grinning beneath the mask.

Ferocious barking awakened Heath, and he groaned at the pain splintering his skull. He rolled over, rubbing the heels of his hands over his eyes. What—where was he?

The area rug in the guest bedroom lay beneath him, and

shards of glass speckled the rug and wood floor beneath it like sharp, shiny stones. Someone had broken in. When he rushed upstairs, he'd been in such a hurry he hadn't taken the time to make sure nothing looked amiss. By the time he flung the guest bedroom door open to get Kara's old camera, it was too late.

The intruder had swung the small garden tool at Heath from behind the door. He'd ducked, but the tool had still clipped his temple and head.

Piper. Laurel. Where were they? Heath leaned against the dresser as a wave of dizziness crashed over him. His stomach lurched, and the pizza he'd eaten earlier threatened to reappear. He held still, drawing in deep breaths for several seconds. Then he pushed off the furniture and scrambled out the bedroom door.

He had to make sure his daughter was okay. Laurel, too. Had to see if the men—

No. *Lord, keep them safe, please. I can't lose Piper.*

Axel and Forge continued raising a ruckus on the deck, their snarling and barking a warning that danger was still nearby. Was it two men or one?

Heath darted down the hallway to the stairs. He changed course and scooted toward the hamper closet, where he kept a firearm tacked high up in the corner inside a lockbox.

He snagged the weapon and tore down the stairs, moving as silently as possible. The man must've climbed to the second floor earlier, when everyone was here, and the dogs were busy searching for scratches and pizza crust. Then he'd ambushed Heath once Axel and Forge were outside.

Heath slipped down to the first floor, the muffled sound of weeping guiding him. He ducked right, opening the back door to the deck. Both dogs bounded in, their fearless energy emboldening him in the terrifying situation. He turned, assessing the living room and kitchen. The front door sat open, allowing cool air to flood his living room. A lamp was upended, ceramic pieces spread on the wood floor near the door. He edged around the corner to look in the kitchen. Lights were off, but he could make out the half-open pantry door. The sobbing noise came from there.

Heath checked his surroundings one more time then rushed into the kitchen and whipped the door wide. Laurel lay in a heap on the ground, blood oozing from a cut on her lip. Rage sizzled down his arms and legs.

Laurel had been manhandled but appeared otherwise unharmed. Where was his daughter?

"Are you hurt?" He crouched, gentling his shaking hands to swipe away a lock of dark hair stuck to the blood on her lip, out of her tear-soaked eyes. "Where is Piper?"

"He…came after us. I t-told Piper to hide in here. When we opened the d-door, the masked man found us and…" A keening sob tore her words apart. "He tried grabbing me. I kicked at him. I h-had Piper behind me, but the shelf fell on us and she…" Laurel closed her red-rimmed eyes. "The stuff fell on Piper, I think it scared her, and she ran past me, out of here. I t-tried to yell at her to come back, but he took her when he heard you moving upstairs."

A furnace spewed flames in Heath's chest.

"Forge and I will get her back." He stood, his muscles bunched like iron bands as he whistled for the lithe canine, who specialized in tracking. "I'm going to leave Axel here." The German shepherd had a bad ACL and couldn't run as far and fast as Forge, but he was a ferocious guard dog. Ninety pounds of teeth and sinew.

"I'm calling backup. They should be here in three or four minutes. Axel, stay," he said forcefully to the German shepherd. "Stay." Then he leaned down and touched Laurel's drawn-up knees. "I'll be back. Help will be here soon."

"I'm so s-sorry, Heath."

"We'll get her back." Had to. There was no choice. "Pray for her, please?"

"Yes. And for you."

He snatched his cell from the coffee table and hit 9-1-1.

"Forge, let's go." He didn't bother with the Dutch shepherd's leash. Forge was well controlled with voice commands, and Heath needed the dog's nose and speed to find his daughter.

Because if he didn't, and soon… He shut the thought down and thundered out his front door, Forge fast on his heels. *God, guide my steps to my daughter. I can't lose her, too.*

ELEVEN

The brisk night air did little to cool the raging inferno inside Heath as he canvassed his front yard. He'd ended the call to dispatch then refocused on the dog. Forge panted excitedly, whining and pacing in circles, as Heath scoured the ground. As far as he could remember, Piper had been wearing a pair of jean shorts and a horse T-shirt. She'd brought her horse blanket down instead of a jacket when—

There. A shiny scrap of brown-and-green material the size of a large beach towel lay rumpled at the end of his driveway, near the mailbox. Lord willing, the man who'd broken in was still on foot.

Heath surged forward and lifted the blanket, offering it to Forge. "Track." The dog sniffed it, very familiar with Piper's scent, but Heath made him sniff it again.

"Good boy. Find Piper," he commanded. "Track Piper." He tucked it under his arm as the dog dropped his keen nose to the ground and took off, directly across the street and into the woods. While he had two houses on his left and three on his right, a twenty-five-acre stand of woods sat in front of Heath's property, undeveloped. He, Piper and Kara had hiked the area a couple of times when Piper was younger. If his memory served him right, about halfway through a creek—a tributary of the Allegheny River—cut through the land. It wasn't deep, but the water was surrounded by mud and hard to pass over.

Forge burst through a hedge and leveled out his gait, cutting through the trees much faster than Heath could. He struggled to keep up with the swift dog on the uneven ground and in the darkness. The half-moon was covered by clouds now. He tugged out the flashlight he'd grabbed in the kitchen and flicked the button. A sharp beam of light sputtered to life, then dimmed.

Great. Low battery. Nothing to do about it now. He held that as he scrambled forward, determined to keep Forge within eye and ear shot.

Two or three minutes of jumping, dodging and pushing through hedges and thickets, and Forge still hadn't barked. How long had he been knocked out? There was a public park and parking lot on the other side of the large section of woods—could the kidnapper have gotten Piper that far?

Please, God. Help us find her. Keep her safe.

Heath almost ran smack into a small, decrepit camping structure that had crumbled and now likely housed bats and teens up to no good in the summertime. He edged around it carefully, the knife wound on his side stinging, then a loud volley of barking sent his arm hair on end.

Found them.

A man's startled cry broke through the night, then an awful, inhuman howling sound followed. Dread skyrocketed up his spine as he rounded the building and launched into the fray.

The masked kidnapper writhed in the mud beside a shallow creek, his body flailing as Forge clamped tight to his right upper arm. Heath had never been bitten by a police K-9, but he had once put on a bite suit to feel the power of the seventy-five-pound dynamos and their clamping jaws and to see how it affected the criminals' trajectory during a chase and takedown.

Heath's gaze lit on Piper, crying and climbing up the bank on the other side of the creek.

"Piper. Get over here!"

"Daddy!" She squealed when she heard him, then dashed over, throwing herself into his midsection like they were playing an intense game of Red Rover, Red Rover.

"I'm here, baby. I'm here." He ran a hand over her damp, sand-coated hair. "I need you to hide over there." He pointed at the structure he'd just edged around. "Wait there for me."

"Daddy, Forge is biting him. Don't let him hurt Forge."

"I won't."

He set her away, behind him, and sprang down the two-foot embankment, landing in slippery mud. The motion was faster than he realized it would be, so he slid forward, nearly losing his footing. Forge's snarls increased as he tugged on the man's arm.

Heath clicked off the safety and settled his stance. "Forge. Release." The dog stopped tugging and whined but held on. Heath repeated it. "Release."

Forge did as he was told. "Come."

The agile animal leaped across the water, just as the criminal tried to rise and run off.

"Hands up!" Heath shouted. "In the air. Higher!"

"Can't. I'm bleeding." The kidnapper hunched over, breathing heavily, and beneath the pale moonlight, a dark stain circled the man's right arm, evidence of the dog's crushing jaws. A strangled moan emitted from Piper's kidnapper.

Heath trod carefully over the stream, cautious of his steps while keeping an eye on the perp. He snatched the handcuffs from his back pocket, drew the man's arms behind his back and slapped them on. The criminal howled at the motion, and

Heath's muscles sagged as soon as he was cuffed. If he wasn't mistaken, this was the man who'd gone after them in the cave.

"Let's go."

"You're not getting anything out of me." The man spat through the mouth hole in his mask, and it struck Heath's jeans. Forge growled.

"Let's go."

Suddenly the bushes snapped behind him, and Heath tensed. Laurel appeared beside the old camp building, holding Piper to her side. Axel panted beside them, loyal to the end and faithfully guarding her.

"What are you doing out here?" he asked more sharply than he intended. The thought of anything happening to her or Piper… He shook his head.

"I had to make sure she was okay." She breathed heavily, shadows hiding her face. He bit his tongue. She was cradling Piper in her embrace, something he couldn't currently do, and he didn't want to make a scene in front of the criminal. A siren's whine carried on the wind. Backup.

Thank You, Lord.

"Move," Heath commanded the kidnapper.

"I didn't even want the kid," the man snapped as Heath dragged him back through the woods to his house. "We were supposed to get *you*." The handcuffed man pivoted and sneered at Laurel, who had fallen into step behind Heath. "You'll never be safe again, lady."

"That's enough." Heath forced the suspect's face forward. Forge trotted beside him, still brimming with energy, while Axel matched pace with Laurel and Piper.

His mind shifted back to the perp's words. Of course, they wanted Laurel. It was indefensible that the criminals were after her. What didn't make sense was why they hadn't been able to reach Tim Polling.

Where was her WITSEC handler, and why hadn't he answered his phone?

They exited the woods just as a police car pulled in, sirens cut. An ambulance followed, its flashing lights blinding them as they trekked across the street into Heath's yard.

Officer Anthony Venetta stepped out of his squad car. "Looks like you had a busy evening."

"Unfortunately, we did," Heath muttered as he shoved the criminal forward.

"I want a lawyer," the suspect snarled, his steps irregular and head rolling on his shoulders. The loss of blood must be affecting him. And if that was the same man from last night, then he also had wounds from their tussle in the cave.

"First thing, you're under arrest for breaking and entering, child endangerment, and kidnapping a minor. You'll get a lawyer once you undergo surgery to close this wound. Then we'll have a long discussion about who you're working for."

"For? For?" the man sputtered. "I work for *me*. I do what I want to do. No one's my boss, on the inside or outside."

Then he slumped to his knees and fell sideways on the grass beside the driveway.

Heath scowled as he helped two paramedics load the heavy man onto a stretcher. They began working on him as they pushed the stretcher into the ambulance, and moments later it drove away.

Laurel huddled with Piper on the front steps, her arms wrapped protectively around his daughter. Axel lay on the walkway at their feet while Forge shuffled around, sniffing the ground, his attention still focused on Heath.

Officer Venetta trotted up the driveway and headed toward Laurel and Piper. "Ms. Bell, did you recognize that man?"

"I didn't see his face, but I did remember his voice." She shuddered. "From the swamp."

"Be right back," Heath told Venetta, then he whistled for Forge and Axel, corralling them through the front door. He grabbed a tennis ball and tossed it to Forge, gave Axel a treat, checked to make sure there was water in both dogs' water bowls, then jogged back outside as Laurel answered questions. Another squad car arrived, and Officer Brett Salido climbed out. Brett was a new young hire from Philly, and his narcotics training and athleticism had been an asset to the Holloway PD.

"Hey, Brett. Thanks for getting here so fast."

"You got him, right?"

"We did. Forge helped." Heath pointed toward the dog, who had followed him out front and now lay in the yard jawing his tennis ball.

"You think this is the suspect that went after her at Black Ash Swamp?" Brett gripped his belt.

"Pretty sure. He also attacked us in the cave at Rimrock last night." He glanced over at Laurel and Piper as Laurel spoke to Officer Venetta. Piper nestled in the circle of Laurel's arms, but when he made eye contact with her, his daughter disentangled herself and ran over to him. He swept her up and held her close, all the emotions he'd kept bottled up inside spilling out. She clung to him, and he slammed his eyes shut so he wouldn't embarrass himself.

"You're safe." He kissed her head then opened his eyes to gaze into her muddy, tear-streaked face. "Anything hurt?"

"Uh uh. You should've seen Miss Laurel. That bad guy got us in the closet and then she hit him with the iced tea container."

"Really?" He and Brett chuckled at Piper's enthusiastic report of what went down in his kitchen earlier.

"Then when he kept coming back, she took the box with the cookie sheets and hit him with those." Piper's eyes rounded. "He tried to get us both, but she threw stuff—even the brownie mix Aunt Molly was going to make brownies with!"

"Miss Laurel is very brave. I'm grateful you're both okay."

Officer Venetta stepped away from Laurel to answer his radio, and Brett edged over in his place to ask how she was doing. The handsome young officer bantered back and forth with her for half a minute, until an unexpected rush of possessiveness heated Heath's veins.

"Brett, would you mind doing a fingerprint sweep of my guest bedroom? First door on your left at the top of the stairs. Watch for broken glass. The suspect breached the window and may have touched the area."

"Yes, sir." Brett sent him a sidelong look then jogged inside, leaving Heath, Laurel and Piper temporarily alone.

Before he could get a word out, another car arrived. This one unmarked. Eli. A year ago, Heath wanted to chase Eli Buchanan out of town when he'd returned to vacation with Skylar. Now his once-estranged high school classmate was a close friend and lifeline, personally and professionally.

Especially right now.

"Eli." Heath waved, relieved to see it was just him and not Molly. Eli and Skylar lived in an older cabin on the other side of Holloway, which Eli had started to remodel. After he and Molly married, she would live with them. For now, and for only a few more days, Molly lived at their dad's house.

"I dropped Skylar off at your dad's earlier. She's having a sleepover with Molly," Eli explained as he treaded over, eyeing Laurel and Piper. "I heard you two had a run-in with the bad guy. Everyone okay?"

Laurel nodded, but her eyes were haunted as she gazed at Piper.

"I got to see Forge get really angry and bite that guy who was pretending to be Batman!"

"Whoa, Batman? Sounds like Forge deserves two tennis balls," Eli joked, and they peered collectively through the dark to where Forge rolled on his back in the front yard, the bright yellow ball stuck near his spine on the grass as he grunted and groaned and tried to smother it.

"Would you mind bringing Piper to my dad's?" Heath asked his friend. "The girls can hang out. I'd feel better that way."

"Laurel, too?"

"Not right now. I want to go over what happened tonight."

"Sure thing."

Heath drummed his fingers against his thigh as they entered his house. What had once been a sanctuary now felt like a war zone because someone had broken in. With the remodeling he was doing of his downstairs guest bathroom, including putting in a new window, he had disarmed parts of the alarm system in the house. And he hadn't rearmed it after they'd come in earlier and eaten dinner. *Not smart.*

These men were determined to get to Laurel. Having her around Piper meant his daughter had gotten caught in the crosshairs…and could again.

He turned and met Laurel's glossy brown eyes. Hers widened as she read his thoughts. The guilt he saw in their depths magnified, expanded, and Heath reached out. "Laurel, wait."

Laurel dashed up the stairs, swiping at the unwanted tears. She'd seen in his devastated expression what was already weighing down her heart with every beat—her presence had put Piper in danger. Grave danger.

She needed to leave. Leave Heath's and leave Holloway.

Tim. Please call me back.

Laurel entered the guest bedroom just as the young, dark-haired officer was leaving.

"Watch out, ma'am. There's glass in there. Sergeant might not want—"

"I won't touch anything."

He nodded then retreated down the stairs, and she stepped inside the room just as a cool breeze wafted in from the window she'd opened earlier. More tears threatened, and the messy room blurred.

This *was* all her fault.

Heath's voice mingled with Eli's at the stairwell. Then Heath climbed the stairs with his daughter, Piper's voice narrating every step and each of her thoughts. Laurel listened to their playful banter as she held her head in her hands. The resilient child had bounced back from the kidnapping attempt, but Laurel hadn't. How could she, when it was her fault Piper was taken?

I can't do this, God. I can't put that sweet girl in danger. Or her dad.

She lifted her head and frowned. Her borrowed cell lay half-hidden on the rug, blinking. Had Tim finally returned her calls? She leaned against the bed frame as Heath's and Piper's voices carried down the hall. Then Heath's steps sounded, closing in, and his broad shoulders filled the doorway.

"What happened tonight is not your fault, Laurel."

She shook her head and glanced past him. Piper must be packing to go with Eli, who was speaking to an officer in Heath's living room, it sounded like.

"It is my fault." She gestured at the window. "When I was taking a nap earlier, I opened the window. I didn't realize..." A sob strangled her apology. "I'm so sorry. Piper could've been—"

"Piper is here. She's safe. You both are."

Laurel cupped her hands over her damp facc. "I'll *never* be safe, Heath. Don't you get it? No matter where I go or what happens, I'll never be safe. Danger will always be around me."

"I'm not stepping away from this investigation."

She dropped her arms then pointed to the phone with trembling fingers. "There's a call on the cell you gave me, but I'm not supposed to touch it, right?"

"Hold on a sec." Heath disappeared into the hall, a door squeaked open, then squeaked shut. He returned wearing two snug yellow cleaning gloves then crouched, grasped the phone and tapped in a code. "Whoa. You have three missed calls, all from the last hour."

She hovered beside him. "Maybe he finally called back."

Heath drew up the main screen of the phone and found the voicemail, then hit play.

"Laurel, this is Alex Vegas, Tim Polling's Director. Please give me a call."

The second message. "Yes, Laurel. Alex Vegas again. It's important that you call me back."

And the third message. "Laurel, Alex Vegas from the San Francisco US Marshals' office. I've been trying to reach you this afternoon. It is imperative we speak immediately."

Heath stared at the phone, then met her rounded eyes. "That's it. Do you know him?"

"No. Tim mentioned Alex a couple times, but I've never met him. Is it too late to call?" She glanced at the alarm clock, which had been knocked to the ground when the man broke in. It said 9:42.

"Call him. He's in San Francisco, they're three hours behind us."

She tapped the number from the message, and it rang twice.

"This is Director Vegas. Is this Laurel?"

"Yes, it is." She perched on the edge of the bed, and Heath joined her. "Where is Tim?"

"We're not sure." The connection crackled. "He left for a solo fishing trip two days ago and hasn't returned. His wife doesn't know where he is, either." He paused, and Laurel's heart slammed into her ribs. Had Tim betrayed her?

She caught Heath's eyes, and the same concern, the same question, echoed in his.

Alex continued. "I hate to be the bearer of more bad news, but August Basile escaped from prison two days ago. The prison guards didn't find out for several hours, and then when the prison official called Tim first, he couldn't get a hold of him. The delay in reaching you is unacceptable, and I apologize."

"Where do you think Tim is?" Tim had been like an uncle to her, a reliable, helpful one who always looked out for her.

"At this time, we don't know," Alex answered. "We're working with his cell phone provider to get that information. I'll fill you in once we find out more."

"But he—Tim—was always available. This isn't like him."

"No," Alex conceded, "it's not. I hate to think the worst, but—"

"You think Tim is working with August Basile?" Heath jumped in.

"To whom am I speaking?" Alex asked sharply.

"This is Sergeant Heath Calhoun with the Holloway, Pennsylvania Police Department. Laurel was attacked yesterday and again this evening. Given the precarious situation, I've been made aware of her past with WITSEC."

"Laurel, is this accurate?"

"Yes, Sergeant Calhoun…has been a huge help. I wouldn't be alive without him."

"I'm deeply apologetic that this happened." Alex sighed.

“That leads to my next point. I’ll need you to come to San Francisco ASAP. We have to get your statement and pull together details about what occurred there and if it was perpetrated by August Basile. I will also write up your new location plans and we’ll figure out where to hide you until August is apprehended. In the meantime, I’ll send a marshal to assist you while you’re traveling so—”

“That’s not necessary,” Heath cut in. “I’ll be accompanying Ms. Bell to your office.” Heath glanced at her for confirmation. She nodded, her mind spiraling with questions as Heath addressed Alex. “I’d like your thoughts on Tim Polling. Is he a reliable agent?”

“Without a doubt, Tim is one of the best handlers we’ve had. He’s watched over half a dozen other WITSEC members with no issues. All are still alive.”

“So, this situation is out of the ordinary?” Heath prompted. “There’s no reason to believe Tim is working with August or anyone else from the Basile Brotherhood?”

“I’ve learned to never say never in this line of work,” Alex returned. “But no, I don’t believe he would betray his oath.”

“When do you need me to come back to San Francisco?” The thought of going home sent an electric shock through her frazzled nerves. She hadn’t been back west in fifteen years, since the Heigels moved to West Virginia to give her a chance at a new life. A fresh beginning.

“As soon as possible,” Alex answered. “Tomorrow if you can manage it.”

Oh, Annaliese. I’m going back. Laurel curled forward. She hadn’t been able to outrun her dangerous past. *The men found me here, too.*

TWELVE

Laurel rubbed the sleep from her eyes as she and Heath plodded through the Pittsburgh airport, which was slowly humming to life at 6:00 a.m.

Heath had called it oh-dark-thirty as they drove through the early dawn fog, away from Holloway.

"It's a five-hour flight. Do you need to use the ladies' room or want anything to drink before we board?" he asked.

Several people mulled around, bleary-eyed like them, offering their phones to airport employees to scan for boarding information. A tall man in a business suit rushed by, apparently already hopped up on coffee.

Speaking of. At his house, Heath had remembered she liked tea and offered to make her some to put in a thermos. All he had in the way of tea bags was black or green, and she'd opted for full-caffeine black tea, which she'd sipped gratefully on their two-hour drive to the airport.

"Yeah, I'd better go before we board."

She searched for a women's bathroom, and Heath accompanied her over to it. They'd spoken very little this morning so far, and her guilt about last night's events weighed heavily on her. He eyed the bathroom door then nudged his chin at the coffee stand across the corridor.

"I'm going to grab something to drink before we get on the plane. I won't be far."

He must be thinking what she did—that whoever was after her wouldn't drive two hours from Holloway to chase her down. Airports were decked out with cameras, and it was a risk she doubted August would take here, in such a public place.

"See you in a minute." She hurried inside. White stalls stretched against the far wall, opposite an equally long line of single sinks set below mirrors. Two women stood in front of sinks, washing hands, and a third woman hovered in the corner, working her hair into a ponytail.

Laurel glanced in the mirror and cringed. Dark circles rimmed her eyes, and her hair was held in a messy bun at the nape of her neck. The light jogging suit she'd borrowed from Molly's closet dragged under her heels because of her shorter height, so Laurel had tried folding the bottoms into cuffs, which just made her appear disheveled.

"Excuse me." A woman brushed past, exiting the bathroom, followed shortly by the one who'd been styling her hair. The remaining woman zipped her purse and left. Suddenly Laurel found herself alone in the long, cavernous room.

As she stepped down the line of stalls to check for a clean one, a blur of motion whipped her head around. Someone with sleek, black hair tucked under a ballcap and oversized sunglasses flew at her from the bathroom door.

Laurel lurched out of reach, but the aggressive woman grabbed the jogging suit with two fists and shoved Laurel into a stall door. Her spine struck the edge, and pain radiated down her legs. She cried out, scrambling to get away from her assailant's clawing grasp. In the process the tiny laceration on her upper lip from the kidnapper's backhand split and stung. But the slight woman rushed at her again, giving her no time to think, shoving a coffee mug in Laurel's face.

"Drink this." The woman flung the liquid at her, and Laurel jerked back as liquid droplets pelted her neck.

"Get off me!" Laurel tumbled onto the toilet, jarring her backside. She kicked at the door so it swung at her assailant, and the motion bumped the mug in her attacker's hand. It flew across the bathroom, clunking into a sink.

A dark, oily liquid spread over the floor like gasoline leaking from a gas station hose.

The woman cursed, then she turned and fled, her hat riding low on her forehead and a flash of light brown hair cascading down the nape of her neck. Was she wearing a wig?

"Heath!" The terminal's music and the increasing noise of the airport must've covered her cry earlier.

She darted out of the stall, avoiding the puddle but crashing into another woman.

"Watch out," the woman snapped, hefting her purse in front like a shield. It was a different woman. Older, shorter, heavyset.

Laurel gaped at the floor and the mug, which had rolled beneath another stall, then ripped off a paper towel and pressed it gently to her throbbing mouth. "Did you see a lady run out of here?"

"The one with the hat on? She almost knocked me over, too. What is happening in here? Are you hurt? I'm going to call the authorities."

"Please do."

"Laurel!" Heath shouted from outside. "Police. I'm coming in."

"Wait, I'm coming out." Adrenaline still pumped through her veins as she rushed out. Heath met her where the men's and women's bathrooms connected and opened into the terminal. She clutched his arm and tugged him farther out into the main hall, looking right and left.

"What happened? Did someone come after you?" He carefully pulled the paper towel from her mouth, and a storm brewed on his face.

"It was a young woman with a black wig on. Hat. Sunglasses. I think her normal hair color is lighter brown. Did you see someone run out of here?"

"I got a call from Chief Lane. They ID'd the perp who kidnapped Piper. Are you hurt?" The concern in his eyes was a balm to her frantic pulse.

"No. It's just the cut from last night. It reopened." She dabbed the wound with the paper towel. "But the woman tried to make me drink from this thermos she was holding."

"I wonder what it was." He blew out frustrated groan. "I'm sorry this happened. I should've stayed right by the door." He leaned close, his big hands gently framing her cheeks as he checked the cut. Heath's featherlight touch set her pulse off for other reasons.

"Who's the man Chief Lane ID'd?"

"Name is Micah Teague." He pulled back then unlocked his cell. "Former heavyweight boxer who trained in California. Got mixed up with some bad people, arrested twice. He was just paroled last month."

"That name doesn't ring a bell."

"No, but he's from the West Coast. Near San Francisco. It's too much of a coincidence. Hold on, I'm calling airport security." A pause. "Yes, my…ah, my friend was attacked in the ladies' restroom in terminal B. Yes." He eyed her up and down. "She doesn't need medical assistance, but we'd like to file a report before we board, see if there's any security camera footage available."

An hour later, after Laurel spoke with the female officer on duty, they boarded their flight. What a scene. As the airport had come to life, hordes of passersby slowed and scoped out the commotion as Laurel detailed what happened. A second officer had appeared, a slim container in his hand to retrieve samples of the liquid that had spread across the tile.

"Looks like coffee but smells kind of weird," the second officer noted.

"They said they'll go over the security cameras in the terminal," Heath murmured after they found their seats. "They'll find something we can use to identify her."

"Problem is, if she took the hat and sunglasses off, she'd look different. Even the hair. I'm pretty sure it was a wig."

"A woman," Heath mused. "Just when we thought it might be August Basile, a woman shows up."

"What if he met a female inmate in prison and told her to come after me once she was released?"

A young man joined the outside seat of their row, interrupting their conversation. Heath adjusted his seat in the middle, his thigh pressing into Laurel's leg as they made room.

"Doubt it," Heath answered once their seatmate donned headphones. "Female and male inmates are kept apart for obvious reasons. Unless it's a girlfriend or former girlfriend of August's and she owes him."

Laurel rested her head against the seat back, one hand capturing a lock of hair and twining it around her finger. Her pulse picked up again as the plane's engines rumbled to life and the wing panels whined open.

"Don't like flying?" He tilted his head so their cheeks were close, his left arm pressing into her right.

"I do it, I just don't think it's natural for a human being to be twenty thousand feet in the air."

"I used to love it, but once we—once I—had Piper, something changed. It felt like a risk. I fly when I have to, once a year to this police conference in Reno, but that's it."

"I'd rather drive. You get to see the land, not just from above."

"Yeah, for sure. Unfortunately, if we drove to San Francisco, we'd be in a car for four days." Heath pulled a face, and Laurel was surprised to realize how much she didn't dislike the idea of spending four days in a car with him.

In fact, despite years of training herself not to get attached to anyone, she had undeniably become attached to Heath Calhoun. Attached to the sense of safety he exuded, but more than that, to him as a person. He cared, truly cared, and it radiated off him in his actions and his words. She'd watched his fellow officers last night, including Eli, and saw how much they respected and trusted him.

"I'm sorry about what happened back there." He tapped his leg repeatedly like he was listening to a music beat.

"It's not your fault. I don't want or need special treatment."

"It's not special, it's for your safety." He turned his face just a bit, and her cheeks flamed at their proximity in the crowded seats and at how secure she felt beside him.

Too safe. Because once they returned, it sounded like Alex Vegas would have new location plans for her. Her eyes stung. Another job. Another city.

God, please keep us safe. Please give us answers about Tim and help them catch August Basile.

Her body quaked, remembering the last time she'd met August's dead-eyed stare in the hushed courtroom where he'd admitted he killed her dad. He'd still worn a bandage on his face that day, and it hit her that the scars from the bullet she'd fired would forever mark his face—and forever give him a reason to want to murder her.

* * *

Heath walked beside Laurel into the San Francisco US Marshals' office, a nondescript two-story building near the Bay. Director Alex Vegas met them in the lobby. A heavyset, older man with an assessing gaze and firm handshake, Alex motioned for them to follow him down the hall.

Heath's stomach dropped, and it wasn't from the bacon and egg bagel he'd inhaled once they landed and were waiting for their rental car. No, this feeling told him something was wrong.

Upon entering the carpeted office with a sign on the door that read, US Marshals, San Francisco Office, Director Alexander Vegas, Alex pointed at two chairs in front of his dark wood desk that made two of Heath's, then sank heavily into his own leather chair.

"Laurel, Sergeant Calhoun. I'm glad you made it safely. First, I wanted to let you know we sent a man in the Pittsburgh area to help local authorities identify and locate the woman who accosted you at the airport. I'm sorry that happened." He removed his glasses and pinched the bridge of his nose before placing them back on. Heath tensed. Something had happened. "I'm afraid I have bad news to share today."

Laurel stilled beside Heath. "About Tim?"

"Yes. California Highway Patrol found Tim's car crumpled along the Pacific Coast Highway, with his body inside."

Laurel slapped her palm over her mouth, and Heath lay his hand on her shoulder and gave a brief squeeze.

"What happened?" He pinned the man with an assessing gaze. As far as he was concerned, no one was innocent in this case. After all, why had it taken Director Vegas so long to reach Laurel?

"Tim was driving along the Pacific Coast Highway, and it appears he ran off the road. His car fell almost one hundred feet and was hidden by trees and bushes at the bottom of a canyon. The CHP used drones to check the area and they… found him."

"He died…in the fall?" Laurel asked.

"We believe so." Alex adjusted his keyboard closer to him. "We're investigating it as an accident, of course, but my coworkers and I are treating it as though it could be otherwise."

Heath leaned forward. "How so? I mean, accidents happen on the Pacific Coast Highway fairly often, correct?"

"That's right, most often caused by weather conditions, but in this case, there are…extenuating circumstances. An alleged car mechanic called our office three days ago, asking for Marshal Polling. A new secretary fielded the call and disclosed that Tim was out of the office on vacation. Headed to Northern California." He frowned. "That information is not supposed to leave our office under any circumstances, of course, but it did."

Laurel seemed to shrink with each of Alex's words. Poor woman. Now she'd lost someone else she cared about.

"What's the next step in Laurel's case? Is she assigned another handler?"

"Eventually, but for now that'll be me. We're short-staffed as it is, and I'll manage her—your—case until this investigation settles and we can assign her to someone I trust."

Heath crossed his arms and gazed at Alex Vegas. The older gentleman would have to earn his trust, not be given it freely.

"Now—" Alex pulled out a small device. A recording tool. "I'd like to go over exactly what happened when you were attacked the first time, and we'll work our way to the events that occurred last night." Alex's gaze jumped from Laurel to Heath, and his countenance clouded over.

Heath knew he was an intimidating guy. Build, experience, all that. He was also aware from research that the

Basile Brotherhood had smuggled guns and laundered money from local businesses. While the heart of the cartel had been brought down by Rodney Campbell's bust and the ensuing arrests, small factions likely still remained. He knew that because they'd dealt with it in northwestern Pennsylvania, too. Drug cartels. A human trafficking front that had been nearly impossible to infiltrate and bring arrests for because former players refused to rat out others for fear of retribution. Criminals banded together, and too often when broken apart, they found other criminals and started new groups.

Even while in jail, August Basile could have reached out and contacted trusted sources, offering payment or goods or protection to entice someone to kill Laurel.

He wiggled his legs as Laurel recounted the events of the last two days. After she wrapped up, her voice reedy, a question struck Heath. "Laurel was cleared of all charges related to shooting August Basile, correct?"

"Absolutely. It was self-defense, plus she was a minor."

Heath glanced her way. Her eyes were damp, hands in a knot, and a stoicism captured her features that he recognized from the first day in the swamp. He didn't like it. It covered the spunky, kind-hearted woman underneath, and he longed to help her to get to a place where she didn't need that mask. Where she felt confident in who she was and didn't have to hide anymore.

"Moving on." Alex regarded Laurel. "The problem we've had all along with August Basile is that he blames your dad—and, by extension, you—for Leonard's death. His father was at the laundromat the day Rodney busted it, and he was one of the three men shot and killed."

"Right," Heath returned. "What happened to August that day he was shot and arrested in Redwood National Park?"

"He was taken to the hospital and underwent extensive surgery."

"Seems like a waste of time and resources," Heath bit out before he could stop himself.

Alex chuckled slightly. "Be that as it may, it still happened. We preferred he live so he could be prosecuted and serve out his life in prison."

"Instead of capital punishment." California had a moratorium on the death penalty, which meant even the hardest and most violent of criminals were gifted extended years of life…unlike Laurel's dad.

Laurel untied her fingers and touched Heath's forearm. Her cooler skin felt like water poured over a fire.

Their gazes sparked together, his dropping to her mouth and the tiny cut marring her lips. He pulled his away because he didn't want Alex Vegas to see too much.

Then he pushed back and stood, pacing the room. "Do you have any way of knowing which state August is in?"

"His tracker was broken off, of course. I do believe it marked him as in the state the first twelve hours after he escaped."

"*How* did he escape?" Heath sank down in the chair again and crossed his arms.

"He and another inmate got into an argument. The other inmate hit him, quite hard, requiring stitches." Alex scowled. "The skin around his eye and left cheek is thin and scarred. It bleeds easily. We think August and the other man were working together, because both were bloodied afterward and sent to the infirmary. August's scars had reopened, and the wound required a more delicate hand than the prison staff had."

"So, he was on his way to the hospital."

"In a manner of speaking. The head warden said they use a surgical clinic about twenty miles from the prison. Someone in the prison must've cut an engine wire on the prison transport van, because the engine overheated halfway there."

"And that's when August escaped."

Alex nodded. "Yes."

Beside him, Laurel shuddered. She had picked at her egg and cheese pita when they'd gotten food earlier, and she likely needed a mental and emotional break after receiving the terrible news about her handler.

A blonde woman poked her head into the office. "Director, Connie Ward is calling from SFPD. She needs to speak to you about the COD."

Alex stood, nodding. "I need to take that. Connie is the medical examiner working on Tim's case."

Heath scratched the back of his neck. The woman likely had information about Tim Polling's body and his cause of death. Another thing Laurel didn't need to hear or know about.

"How about I take Laurel for a bite to eat, then we'll get settled at the hotel. What time would you like to meet back up?"

Alex flipped through his phone as he came around the desk. "Three o'clock work? Then I can take you two out for dinner at the best crab restaurant on the Bay."

Heath choked down a sarcastic retort. Laurel didn't need to be wined and dined. She needed to give her deposition and get out of here. Being back in San Francisco clearly wasn't good for her.

It hit him like a ton of bricks how much he cared about what was, and wasn't, good for her.

Don't go there, Calhoun. He followed her out of Alex's office, his thoughts snagging on the memory of Kara's last day. Hearing the doctor admit—after his wife flatlined—that the second pregnancy might've taxed her heart enough to draw out the genetic abnormality.

Heath groaned as they made their way to the building's lobby and main doors.

"You okay?" Laurel turned to him.

"Leave it to you to ask that after all you've been through."

She slowed her steps at the front doors. The secretary was on the phone, and the marshals' office was tomblike, as most people were at lunch. "What do you mean?"

"You just had to recount the worst day of your life. Most people would be focused on themselves, their own pain. Not you. You're worried about me."

She shook her head. "No, things have changed."

He drew back. "What do you mean, they've changed?"

"The day my dad was shot was awful. The worst day of my childhood, hands down. But last night? When Piper was taken by that man, and I knew it was because of me?" Her features sank. "*That* was the worst day of my life."

Heath didn't care. He just went with it, engulfing Laurel to him, moved by her downcast demeanor and the way she cared about his daughter despite barely knowing Piper or him.

"You said you feel so weak." Heath rested his chin gently on her head, which fit neatly against his chest. "But all I see is a person who survived a terrible ordeal and came out stronger and still cares about others above herself."

She held still within his embrace, her small form shaking like a leaf.

Someone cleared their throat, and Laurel pulled away and averted her face as Alex Vegas approached, his face ashen.

"I'm sorry to interrupt, but the coroner had additional news." Alex's gaze took in Laurel's emotional state then focused on Heath. "While the fall from the highway certainly would've been fatal, it appears that Tim Polling was shot before he hit the guardrail and went over."

"He was shot," Heath repeated slowly.

"I'm afraid so. The bullet is being sent to the SFPD forensics lab."

Heath thanked Alex, gently gathered Laurel against him, and headed to the rental. Everything pointed to the undeniable fact that August Basile or his fellow criminals had probably taken out the WITSEC handler to give themselves time to get to Laurel.

Now only Heath stood in the way of them killing her.

THIRTEEN

"You're sure you don't need something to eat?" Heath asked Laurel again.

"I don't really have much of an appetite, but we can stop if you're hungry." They were driving through her old neighborhood, and the sights and sounds—and smells—of the Bay Area she had once loved both pulled at and repelled her.

Bittersweet emotion overwhelmed her as she took in their surroundings. Once she'd dreamed of coming back here, setting down her roots like her grandparents and her parents had. But now it felt like she was driving over the surface of the moon, and she was familiar with the surroundings from pictures, but that was it.

Her emotional connection to this place only existed in memory now.

Especially after receiving the terrible news about Tim. She closed her eyes and rubbed her eyelids. Willing away the ache at the back of her skull and the dull throbbing in her chest.

She couldn't stop thinking about how safe, how *right* it felt when she'd been in Heath's arms. She'd needed the comfort, and his strength had anchored her when she very nearly collapsed.

Tim was dead, and it wasn't an accident. August Basile was loose. Running rampant, causing death and destruction just as he had before. When she was a child and had to testify before the judge about her dad's murder, she'd overheard a conversation between two of the lawyers. They'd been busy and distracted, unaware Laurel's curious, young ears were perked and her confused mind groping for more about what had happened that awful day her dad was killed.

You know, August is the black sheep in the Basile family, one of the female lawyers said.

How so? the other lawyer, a man, had asked.

At least Leonard Basile was a reasonable criminal, the woman replied. *He killed for financial gain and dominance, not sport. But August? That young man is psychopathic. No remorse. Did you hear about that girl he—*

The noise in the courtroom had increased, cutting off Laurel's ability to hear the rest of their mutterings. Which, as an adult, she realized was a blessing. Because even twenty years later, her memories of August's hateful sneer and cold eyes when he'd fired that gun hadn't dimmed.

"Anything good to eat around here?"

She shook off the memory, grateful for the disruption of her dark thoughts. "Didn't we just eat three hours ago?"

"Yeah, but I got up early, so I have the munchies."

"Do you like seafood?"

He twitched. "Hard pass. Molly peer-pressured me into eating salmon a time or two, but I much prefer land animals over scales and gills. How about you?"

"I used to love seafood. Dad and I went out to Fisherman's Wharf once a month or so. Mom, too, but those memories are fuzzier."

"I'm sure I can find a burger or chicken at a fish restaurant."

"There is this one little place. It's Italian." She'd only known

Heath a few days, but she recognized a pattern. "You can get calzones, pizza, chicken parmigiana—"

"Chicken parm? Now you're speaking my love language."

She smiled, and then gave him directions to Antonio's, a mom-and-pop diner that had the best Italian around. Ten minutes later, they arrived. Heath scoped out the parking lot and walked right beside her as they entered, and she noticed that he asked for a table by the window, then sat so he could keep an eye on their rental car.

They'd just received their drinks and placed orders when Heath turned and regarded her with a simmering look that made her cheeks flush.

"Do you trust Vegas?"

"I don't have any reason not to at this point." She unfolded her fork and knife from the wrapped napkin. "What about you? You don't?"

"I'm about eighty percent confident he's being honest. It takes a couple impressions before I'm at one hundred percent."

"I only ever talked to him one other time, when Tim went on vacation last year." Her fork clattered to the table. "I can't believe he's gone."

"I'm sorry." Heath reached across the booth and clasped her unsteady hand.

"This is all because of me and my dad's murder." She stared out the window, taking in the familiar buildings and sights and hating how frightened it made her feel.

"Tim is dead because a criminal killed him. Not because of you. If it hadn't been someone from your dad's case, it could've been someone from another case. It's a dangerous line of work."

She returned her gaze to his. "Did you really research my dad's death and the investigation?"

He shrugged sheepishly. "I was interested in it when I was a kid, but wasn't allowed to see any of those behind-the-scenes details. Now, especially because of you, I want to know all of it. Every detail." He leaned forward, his large hand encircling her wrist and part of her knuckles. She relished the sensation of being cradled. Of being cared for. "Your dad cut off the head of the snake, but unfortunately there was a nest nearby with babies. And August Basile is the most dangerous of those. So we take out the nest."

She shuddered at that imagery.

"Sorry, I can be a little…"

"Intense. Eli was right. You're an excellent person to have on my case." His face flushed at her praise.

"I mean, I feel strongly that once he's caught, you'll be safe and you can finally…live a normal life. Not be scared all the time. You of all people deserve that."

"Thank you." She flipped her hand over, so their palms met, then she threaded their fingers. His dwarfed hers, and a sense of security and peace reassured her. Heath cared. He really cared. He wanted to help.

He looked down at their twined hands. His darker, tan fingers and her lighter, slender ones. A shadow crossed his brow. He was thinking of Kara. How forward of her to encroach on the special love they had by—

"I'm sorry." Laurel disentangled their fingers and brought hers to her lap. "I shouldn't have done that."

"Nah, it's okay."

The waitress arrived, holding Laurel's chicken Caesar salad and Heath's chicken parmigiana. She made sure they were all set, then hurried away to another table.

"Mind if I bless the food?"

"Yes, please." They both bowed their heads, but he didn't offer her his hand this time.

"Dear God, thank You for this food. Please bless it to our bodies, watch over our loved ones and keep us safe here and on the way home. In Jesus' name, amen."

"Amen." She lifted her drink and downed a sip of water, watching with a small smile as he dug into his plate. He hadn't been kidding about his enthusiasm for chicken parmigiana.

An hour later they drove through her old stomping grounds. The elementary school she'd attended, her favorite bike path near the Bay. The hospital where she'd been born. The imposing Golden Gate Bridge sat in the background, a reminder of her dad with every heartbeat, every glance.

She motioned. "Want to drive over that big old bridge?"

Heath's grip on the wheel intensified. "Another hard pass."

"Wait, is this another quirk?" she teased.

"Yeah, well, I am *not* a fan of big bridges. All those movies I watched when I was younger scarred me for life. You know, where the monster grabs the bridge and breaks it apart, or an earthquake rattles the area, the bridge splits and the cars careen into the water? Yeah, no thanks."

A tenderness swelled in her heart for this tough guy who hid real fears of his own. "I won't tell. We can drive up beside the Bay and take some pictures of it for Piper and Molly instead, if you'd like, before we head back to the US Marshals' office."

"That I can handle."

"Oh, before we do that." She scrutinized their surroundings. "Did you want to see the laundromat where Dad busted the BB?" She pointed to the left, and Heath clicked on his turning signal. Once they turned and he straightened the wheel, she counted off older buildings, a rush of anxiety tightening her rib cage. *There.* She pointed to a mint-green, one-story building on the right, the words *Calypso Spa* emblazoned across the front.

"People go there to get pedicures now, but once it was a fake laundromat and the main drop-off point for the biggest criminal in San Francisco for the last thirty years."

Heath slowed as they neared the building, fitting their rental car neatly into a parallel spot across the street. "Looks like every other building here."

"Yes. They painted it since I last saw it. Changed the windows, and the door appears new. It looks…different." Almost like several men weren't injured or killed here, in the back room.

"Was August there that day?"

"No." The word came out sharper than she intended. "Leonard Basile had several associates there, and his older son, Matteo. Matteo was shot and killed along with Leonard, but two associates lived. One man ran and was never caught."

"Do authorities know who it was? They're sure it wasn't August who took off?"

"August was nineteen that year. He was at the family compound in Sacramento, although he disappeared after the arrests here."

"So, he saw your dad's name on the news and plotted his revenge."

She tipped her chin forward until it touched her chest. "Yes. He must've figured out Dad and I biked at Redwood. He followed us and…"

Heath was silent for long enough that Laurel lifted her head to catch him frowning at the rearview mirror. He put the car into Drive, checked traffic and pulled back onto the road.

"Heath, what is it?"

"I've seen the same car drive by three times now. I could be wrong, but I believe we're being tailed."

They'd been followed to the airport—did that mean August's henchmen were coming after them *here*, too?

"I'm going to drive normally, like I have no idea, but I want you to reach down and grab my cell from the console. See it? Yes."

She leaned forward and did as he asked, and her chest tightened as she inputted his code.

"Good." He sped up slightly, and she almost bumped her forehead into the dash of the modest-sized rental. "Go to my contacts and pull up Alex. He should be near the top."

She thumbed through his cell and located the Director's number. "I found it. Are they still there?"

"I lost them once we turned right, but I see them again. Black SUV, looks like a Secret Service vehicle."

"But it's not?"

"I'm sure it's not. Call Alex and stay down, please."

Laurel drew up the contact and waited, her heart thumping into her ribs. Several rings later, it went to voicemail. Why wouldn't anyone answer their phone?

"No answer." Her breathing picked up at the severe look on his face.

"Hit 9-1-1, tell them who I am and where we are."

She did as he told her, sputtering out their whereabouts to the dispatcher then hanging up. She poked her head up just far enough to take in their surroundings, then gasped.

They were traveling on Highway 101, boxed in by traffic—heading straight for the Golden Gate Bridge.

Heath wove around traffic as he tried to lose the black Cadillac Escalade with dark tinted windows. Sweat gathered on his brow, and his legs jiggled faster with each passing moment. The vehicle chasing them looked new and loaded, and it was impossible to see the driver or passenger.

"Stay down." His damp palms slid on the steering wheel as they neared the famous suspension bridge that was the thing of his nightmares. Traffic was surprisingly light, and they approached much too quickly. No turnoffs so far.

He gritted his teeth as they entered the lanes to cross the massive orange-reddish structure that he'd watched get ripped apart on the big screen too many times. It spanned a mile over San Francisco Bay, and there was no way to avoid it now without getting into a major accident.

God, I really need Your help with this. He strangled the steering wheel and continued forward. Up ahead, blinking road work signs flashed.

They were traveling twenty over the speed limit. Fellow drivers glared at him as he sped past, pushing the four-cylinder engine as hard as it would go. He hated to do it, but at least if a cop clocked him and—

"Heath, look out!" Laurel screamed as a van changed lanes right in front of them.

He veered to the left, and Laurel bounced toward him before her seat belt caught. His left leg slapped into the driver's side door as he straightened and zoomed ahead in the left lane. Only a couple of hundred yards left until they were on top of the bridge. Up ahead a large orange sign loomed, an arrow pointing to the right. He had to merge and soon. Behind him, the hulking SUV charged, shadowing his every lane change.

"Hang on." He slammed the brakes so the car on their right could get far enough ahead he wouldn't crash into them when he merged.

A *ping, crack* echoed in the car, and Laurel screamed. Shiny shards of glass rained over the dash.

"Stay down!" He jerked the steering wheel, honking loudly at the sports car to his right. "Police! Out of the way."

The cherry-red sports car finally slowed as they entered the bridge, and Heath's muscles froze as glittering miles of water spread out on both sides of the vehicle. *Don't look, don't look.* The construction occurred about halfway across the bridge, which meant he only had a minute or so to figure out how to lose the Cadillac.

"Are they still there?" Laurel cried.

"Yes, but we're about to slow down. Hold on."

He hit the brakes again, and the little sedan squealed as they came within inches of the stopped vehicle in front of them. At the last second, he maneuvered around it, grateful he hadn't rented an SUV. The car he drove was hardly bigger than a dune buggy, and Heath used that to his advantage as he raced alongside the line of orange cones, sending a few flying. Horns honked and rude gestures were flung, but he didn't care.

They had to lose the SUV.

He glanced behind them. The Cadillac pulled a U-turn in a spot meant for law enforcement. His shoulders loosened, and his stranglehold on the steering wheel went slack.

"Thank the Lord, they're turning around."

Heath slowed the car and drew in a measured breath, but it didn't alleviate the black hole opening in his chest. *Water, water, everywhere.* He was on a bridge. A huge, mile-long bridge. His heart pounded and sweat dampened his back.

"Are you okay?" She checked behind them before staring at Heath, a worried expression on her face.

"Not really."

"Do you want me to drive?"

"Thanks, but I can do this." A siren carried over, and flashing blue lights zoomed toward them from the construction farther down the bridge. A uniformed officer parked then strode over.

Each second felt like an eternity.

"Sir, you were speeding and driving recklessly. License and registration."

Heath held his hands out so the tall, thin young man could see them. "Officer, I'm a sergeant with the Holloway Police Department in Holloway, Pennsylvania. My passenger, Laurel Bell, just called 9-1-1 because we were being tailed after we left the US Marshals' office on Planter Street earlier. I sped in order to outrun the black SUV tailing us. We need an APB on a black Cadillac Escalade, newer model. Dark-tinted windows."

"You have ID?"

"Yes, I'm going to grab it from the compartment here. I also have a weapon registered in my name." He pointed to the glove compartment, then slowly reached down to pull out his wallet and his gun. "My name's Heath Calhoun. Call US Marshal Alex Vegas. He's the Director of the San Francisco Marshal Office. Here's his card."

The officer eyed the weapon then Laurel. "You all right, ma'am?"

"I am now. The SUV shot at us. See the hole and the glass?" She pointed to the back window. The officer's mouth went slack. Laurel's expression faltered as she glanced at Heath. She must've read the discomfort on his face at being stuck in the middle of the huge bridge.

"Sit tight." The officer took Heath's license and disappeared into his squad car.

"Can we ask him if we can get off of here?"

"No, no." He ground his jaw. "This is helping me overcome my fear of bridges."

"It looks like you're about to get sick."

"I am *okay*. I will *be* okay." He tried convincing himself as much as her with his overemphasized comment.

"Do you think we have to go to the San Francisco police station?" Laurel clutched her knees.

"Possibly." He turned, catching her eye. She didn't want to

go to the station. It troubled him how quickly he'd learned to read her thoughts through her lovely eyes and facial gestures. She must've spent time there after her dad was murdered.

"I just want to go to my hotel room and lie down."

Heath reached over, gave her arm a quick squeeze, distracting himself as much as her.

The young police officer returned. "Everything checks out. Welcome to San Francisco, Sergeant Calhoun. Ma'am."

"Heath. And this is Laurel."

The officer extended his hand. "I'm Officer Engleman. Call me Danny. I'll escort you to the station to give your statements."

Laurel moaned.

"Can you ask your superior if we can go back to our hotel and rest first? Ms. Bell is exhausted—we both are from the early flight and that car chase—and we could use some rest beforehand."

Thirty minutes later they pulled into a four-story white-and-gray hotel. Inside rooms. Heath's muscles eased, and he parked, then rubbed the knots from his neck. The rush of adrenaline from the car chase and then from sitting on that bridge had cleaned him clear out, and he could use a nap.

"I can come back in an hour or so," Danny noted as he walked with them into the hotel lobby toward the front desk. He addressed Laurel. "What do you think of the city? Bit different from back east."

"I'm actually from here."

"Really. Whereabouts?"

"I grew up in Noe Valley. My dad worked for SFPD."

"Small world. Where's he work now?"

Heath grimaced, glancing at Laurel. Her features held perfectly still beneath that indifferent mask she wore, except for her eyes and the slant of her slender brows. He knew how to read them now, and he cupped her elbow.

"He was killed a long time ago."

"Oh man, I'm sorry I brought that up." Danny's face flushed red.

"It's okay. My dad was a hero." Her shoulders rose slightly. "I'm proud of him."

Heath let go of her elbow, gathered the key cards from the receptionist, thanked her, then the trio started toward the elevator.

"Do you mind me asking his name?" Danny held out his hands. "I've only been on the force for five years, but I'm from the area, too. Hayes Valley."

She met Heath's eyes. Was it okay to share who he was? Heath nodded then shrugged.

"Detective Rodney Campbell."

"No way. He's a legend around here." Danny stared at Laurel. "You're his daughter? Word is the man who killed him is on the loose. Basile's younger son, that sick—"

"We know," Heath interrupted. "That's why we're here."

"I'll talk to my superior, see if I can stick with you two for the remainder of my shift. That is, if you need an extra set of eyes."

"That would be great, thanks," Heath answered.

Ten minutes later he and Laurel were settled in their rooms. There was a door connecting them, and Heath stood there, debating whether to leave it half-open or shut it as Laurel collapsed on her bed.

He heard her sit up. "Please don't shut it. Knowing you're there…gives me peace."

His chest warmed, but he shook off her words. *Don't even think about it, Calhoun.* Laurel would be leaving. Not now, maybe, but *soon.* After this case was settled, and Lord willing, August Basile was caught, Laurel Bell would have to relocate. Start a new life.

And that was that. "Do you need anything?" he called.

She didn't answer for a long while, so long he thought she might've fallen asleep already. But then her honeyed voice carried over. "A life without fear."

He smiled, but it felt pained. "I pray you get that."

"And a life with a lot of love."

"I pray—" he swallowed "—you'll get that, too."

"What about you? What can I pray for, for you?"

He closed his eyes, his muscles twitching as they rested. Sleep tempted him, and because of that, he spoke without thinking. "That I learn how to forgive the unforgivable."

Kara. *I'm so sorry, baby.*

Another bout of silence followed, and he was suddenly wide awake. Wondering what she made of those cryptic words. Then he heard rustling and the pad of bare feet. Laurel peeked through the half-open doorway, her hair tumbling around her shoulders, her petite frame swimming in Molly's green warm-up suit.

"What do you mean?" She tiptoed over and sank onto the bed beside his.

"Kara died because of me." He was so tired, he didn't care about sharing his big, bad secret. The one that kept him up at night and distorted his happiest moments with Piper.

"*This* is the sadness in your eyes," she whispered. "You believe her death is your fault."

"I don't believe it. I know it."

His feet moved back and forth over the white comforter at the foot of the bed, his ankles cracking as he tried to organize his thoughts and the complicated emotions from the loss of his beloved wife nearly two years ago.

"Kara knew she had a family history of heart issues, but

they had never affected her life or her parents. She figured it might be a problem later in life, not when she was thirty years old. Her pregnancy with Piper was picture perfect." His mind clouded over. "But I really wanted another child. Or two more, even. Kara knew that, and the giving person she was, she didn't want to stop trying. So, we ended up getting pregnant again, and then it was…"

"What?" Laurel pressed softly.

"It was too late. According to the doctor who did Kara's postmortem, the pregnancy taxed her heart function, and it just… I lost her. And the baby was…too little. He died, too." He swiped at his eyes. "The only mercy was that we hadn't told Piper her mom was expecting. So at least…" He groaned. "At least I didn't have to tell her she lost her mom and her little brother."

Laurel moved over to sit down beside him. Her hand found his, twining them together. "I'm so sorry, Heath. That's a double loss. Double heartache."

"We'd chosen the name Benjamin for him. Ben."

"What a nice, strong name."

"I can't help thinking that Kara felt betrayed in those last minutes of her life. I was at work and couldn't make it right away. She was gone by the time I got there." He shoveled his free hand over his face and glared at the ceiling. "A burglary! I missed saying goodbye to her because I was trying to solve a home invasion crime. What kind of husband am I?"

"A loving one. I have no doubt Kara knew how much you loved her. Every time you talk about her, it's obvious you adored—adore—her."

"You know what I hate the most?" Heath whispered, not waiting for Laurel to answer before continuing. "I hate that life keeps moving even though your loved one isn't there to move right along with it. No new memories to share, just the past. It's like you're forced to ride on an escalator, and they get off before you. But the escalator keeps moving, you keep moving, even though they're left behind."

"I think you and Piper will always keep Kara close. I love the pictures you have up, and the way you talk about her." Laurel leaned so their arms brushed. "You have to forgive yourself, Heath. You can't condemn what God ordained."

"What?" He startled. "Say that again? Please."

"*You can't condemn what God ordained.* Annaliese used to tell me that. Yes, I'd had a difficult, painful life, but she would gently remind me that there was much beauty still to come."

"My dad said that to me, too. About what God ordains." He gripped her hand. "But that doesn't always keep the anger away. Toward the situation. Toward God for allowing it to happen."

"I know. It feels like there's a limit to what He can take from each person, and He reached that limit before I turned ten." She sniffled. "I'm grateful Dad left the Heigels in his will as guardians. They were a lot older, but they were kind, and patient. I was angry, you know? And they just kept at it about God. About His faithfulness. I mean, their only son had been murdered, and yet they still believed. They weren't bitter. Annaliese must've recognized that I needed to forgive Him for that perceived wrong." She covered a yawn. "Guess we both have some work to do."

"I have a feeling it's a lifelong process."

She yawned again, and Heath sat up. "How's your lip?"

"Sore, but okay." She fingered the tiny round Band-aid overtop the cut.

"C'mon. Let's get you some sleep." He walked her back to her room. "We have to be out of here in an hour, first to the police station then back to meet Alex. He texted and said changing our meeting time to four was fine."

"See you in a bit." He heard her go into the bathroom, and the door shut, then Heath did the same. As he splashed warm water over his face and stared in the mirror, a prayer hovered in his mind's eye.

I give it all to You, Lord. Kara's death, this situation. All of it. I can't do this on my own. Heath swiped the water droplets from his face with the hand towel and glared at his blurry reflection. *And help me keep these feelings for Laurel in check. The last thing she needs to deal with is a new relationship, even if that's what I want.*

As he padded back to the bed and flopped down, Heath couldn't help wondering if she wanted that, too.

FOURTEEN

She and Heath sat in the matching chairs in Alex's office late that afternoon. She'd napped heavily for an hour, dreaming of the redwoods and her mom's smile and tasting the famous sourdough bread from Biermen's Breads that she, her dad and Mom made sandwiches with after church on Sundays in summer.

The memories were fleeting but powerful, and she'd awoken with damp cheeks and a heavy heart. Heath had been quiet on the drive in, vigilant with checking the rearview mirror.

"Have you learned anything else about Tim?" she asked right away.

"Nothing new, I'm afraid. The coroner is finishing up her report today. She recovered the bullet and sent it to the lab." Alex leaned back in his chair, reminding her of Heath doing the same thing the first day she met him. It felt like a lifetime ago, yet it was only a couple of days past.

"There is something else we need to go over before you head to the airport tomorrow morning." Alex slid a cursory look her way. "Because of August's situation, and the fact that he knows where you are, I've put in for relocation on your case."

She dug her nails into the arm rest. Since that first attack at the swamp, she'd had a terrible feeling Holloway would become a town she'd have to think about in memory. Part of her past instead of her future. "What if he's caught? Can I stay in Holloway then?"

"I'm not promising anything." Alex clicked his mouse and frowned at whatever he saw on the screen. "Because we don't have August in custody—yet—and there are others working with him, it's best to get you to a new location under a new alias."

Laurel clenched her eyes shut as the room spun. Not only a new location but a new name? She wrapped her arms over her middle, which felt hollow and empty like her heart.

"My guess is August just wanted revenge, but he didn't want to give away his cover," Heath noted. "So, he used a couple prison acquaintances—people he's blackmailing, maybe—to go after her. Once they're all arrested, surely she can resume her job and remain in Holloway?"

"As I said, I can't promise that."

"Director," Heath tried again. "I think Laurel and I have earned an in on this situation." He leaned forward. "Where is August Basile?"

"We don't know at this point." Alex pushed away from his desk and rubbed his palms together. "We believe August is the last wild card from the original cartel. Two other wanted criminals tied to Leonard Basile turned up in Wyoming and were apprehended about six months after Rodney Campbell was—after he was killed." He flicked through the papers on the desk. "Micah Teague and Angelo Costa."

"Micah Teague? We just arrested him in Holloway." Heath's face went slack. "My chief ID'd him early this morning. He attempted to kidnap Laurel and took my daughter instead, last night. He's in custody at Holloway General after my K-9 officer brought him down."

Alex's eyes widened, then he nodded slowly, pleased. "Excellent. We believe Micah is the criminal who escaped the day your dad busted the cartel. He was a young man, in training under Leonard. Maybe only nineteen or twenty." He addressed Heath. "I'll need your supervisor's name. As I was saying, Teague and Angelo Costa served ten years and twelve years, respectively, for drug trafficking and money laundering. Both were released on good behavior a few years ago."

Laurel straightened. "So, Micah already knew August then?"

"Quite likely, although we have no record of Teague or Costa leaving California or staying in touch with August."

"How can you know for sure?"

"We have our sources and ways," Alex demurred. "But it's worth checking, especially now that you have Teague in custody." He typed rapidly for several seconds.

"So August and these men coming after Laurel aren't necessarily still active members of the Basile Brotherhood," Heath contemplated. "They could be going after her for another reason. Say, just for revenge from what happened to them at the laundromat." Heath rubbed his cheek. "I'm not sure we mentioned this earlier, but the man who set Laurel's cabin on fire also nabbed a picture of her and her dad from a photo album in the cabin. Don't you find that suspicious?"

"Ah, yes, if you're certain the picture was taken by the man, then it could very well hold up as evidence if we locate it again."

Heath continued. "Can we track where this other man is, Angelo Costa? Do you have their mug shots?"

"Currently working on that, though I would guess they've assumed alternate identities for travel."

Laurel clasped a loose lock of hair and wound her finger through it. Could the remaining members of the BB cartel have gotten in touch with August in prison? A memory sparked.

"When I was testifying, I remember one of the lawyers mentioned a foundation. What happened to the Basile Foundation after Leonard was killed and August went to prison? There was no immediate family left, correct?"

"That's right," Alex answered. "Because August was convicted of first-degree murder, he was unable to access the foundation's money while incarcerated."

"Where did it go?" Heath asked. "The funds."

"Well, the FBI seized the accounts immediately after the cartel was busted." Alex squinted at the screen, then whistled. "Looks like three hundred and twenty million dollars still sit in the trust." He frowned. "Hold up. There is one family beneficiary."

Heath set his palms on Alex's desk. "Who?"

"It appears Leonard Basile had a half sibling, born to his father much later in life. From an affair. There's a son. Damien Basile. Never mind, he's deceased. Huh. But..."

Laurel's mind whirred at this news.

"Right now, no one is receiving the money from the foundation. The state has control. But there appears to be a trust fund set up for any living relatives, with a cool fifty-thousand-dollar payout each month."

"And who is receiving that money?" Heath asked.

"No one has until recently. A couple of months ago, the checks began clearing to an Ellen Basile after she was added to the account. Look at that. It appears August Basile has a cousin in her late twenties."

"Did he just recently find out about Ellen, or had he known about her before?" Heath mused.

Laurel's mind rewound to the airport bathroom, and her skin turned clammy. "Does she have a petite build, like my height, skinny?" Although it had been hard to tell under the belted trench coat, wig, hat and glasses.

"There's no physical description, just a small picture of her driver's license." Alex's dark eyes widened, and he spun his monitor around and pointed at something on the screen to Heath. "Is that near Holloway?"

Heath glared at the monitor then exhaled. "You've got to be kidding me. His cousin lives in Franklin, Pennsylvania."

"How close is that to Holloway?" Laurel vaguely remembered driving by a Franklin on her way to Holloway the day she first moved there but couldn't place its exact location.

"Franklin is about an hour south." Heath glanced at her, his eyes narrowing as he took in the Band-aid on her lip. "How did he get there so fast, and who came after us earlier today?"

"If they hitched a ride on a train, cargo truck or eighteen-wheeler, you can cross the country in two or three days," Alex noted.

Laurel fused her spine to the hard leather seat. "*I* can't get to the money. So does he just want revenge?" She looked between the two men, both deep in thought, once again feeling unmoored and alone despite Heath sitting beside her.

Yes, he'd protected her, stayed by her side through the worst circumstances this week. Through her weakness, God used Heath to make her stronger. But as the target of August Basile's revenge rage, any dangerous situations that affected Heath would be through association with her. And then there was sweet Piper. Laurel sagged forward.

"Given the situation and what's already occurred, I do believe it's in your best interest to go into hiding until August is apprehended."

"I've promised Heath's sister that I'd take pictures of her wedding rehearsal and the ceremony the next day. It's this weekend. I can't… I don't want to miss that."

"We can figure something else out," Heath said warily. "Your life is not worth a few pictures."

"You can protect me, Heath." She ran her fingers across her chin, hating the thought that she couldn't at least thank the Calhoun family for their kindness with this one gesture of gratitude. Her gift for seeing beauty in the ashes of life through her camera lens. "Please, let me do this, then I'll come back here." She addressed Alex. "Or go wherever you think is safe."

"Well, I wasn't thinking you'd come back here, exactly," Alex replied. "We've been in touch with an associate who makes placements. He found a spot in Alabama. Small town on the coast. It would be the best answer for—"

"Alabama?" Heath sputtered.

Alex flung one hand out. "It's the safest spot at the moment. Otherwise, we take her out of the continental US, and that's a logistical nightmare for the department."

Heath's mouth tightened, but he didn't say anything else.

"Watch over her for the next two days, then we'll get her away from Holloway. Away from August Basile." Alex's assessing gaze bounced back and forth between them. "Can you do that?"

"Yes. I will." Heath straightened, his arm pressing hers on the armrest, a reminder of his faithful nature and how much she wished they…

Stop it, Laurel. He was doing this as an officer of the law. And as a caring man.

That was it.

"I'll keep her safe until we catch the suspect," Heath promised, but his statement didn't wipe the grim expression from Alex's face or the dread rooting deep in her heart.

Heath strode closely beside Laurel as they entered the Pittsburgh Airport's parking garage. Unlike their flight out yesterday, the place was bustling with activity. He had hooked his left arm through her right upon deboarding, and now he scrutinized their surroundings critically.

"You mind this?" he'd asked about his close proximity and protective arm.

"No." Her voice had been sad. "I know you're trying to keep me safe."

It's about more than that now.

It was one of the reasons he needed to watch himself. Because he loved big, and as Molly always said, he needed to make sure he ended up with a woman who loved as big as he did. All out. One hundred and ten percent. Kara had. And it was becoming clear that Laurel did, too.

He couldn't deny it. She was a person who cared deeply, and that both pleased and scared him.

They hadn't spoken much on the early flight; instead he'd gone through his work emails and checked voicemail for Chief Lane's updates about the case. He'd notified Lane about what Alex had found, and Chief had been in touch with local Franklin authorities as well as a district judge to obtain a search warrant for Ellen Basile's house.

Fifteen minutes later they'd pulled out of Pittsburgh, heading north on 79 in his truck. He took in the familiar, rolling hills as they drove away from the city, and every few seconds he checked the rearview mirror.

His phone buzzed, and he hit the speaker button. "Calhoun here."

"It's Chief Lane. I have some updates. First, where are you and Ms. Bell?"

"We're on 79, heading back to Holloway."

"Good." Chief Lane cleared this throat. "The man who set Laurel's cabin on fire was pulled over near Corry. Speeding, no tags on his vehicle. Three empty containers of cooking oil in the trunk. He's at the station for questioning."

"Excellent. Do you have a name?"

"We do. Angel Costa. Also has another alias, Angelo."

Heath whooped. "Micah Teague and Angelo Costa are the two men Director Vegas said might be connected to August. I'm thinking there must be at least one or two other suspects, the men who followed us to the bridge in San Francisco. I'd guess they were also incarcerated around the same time and place as August. Let's talk to prison officials and check names, see who was released and stayed in that area."

"Right." Chief Lane paused as though jotting down notes.

"Any word about the woman at the airport?" Heath asked.

"Airport authorities confirmed the ID through facial recognition software from the parking lot camera. Ellen Marie Basile of Franklin."

"Yes," Heath murmured, drawing out the word. "We got her."

"Not quite yet. Did you say in your message that you're joining the Franklin PD at Ellen's house?"

"I did." Heath glanced at Laurel, who now faced him, her eyes rounded. "I want to be there if August is apprehended." He wanted to find and throttle the man who had targeted Laurel and her dad in the first place.

They ended the call, and he set his cell down.

"We're stopping in Franklin?"

"I want to be there when they question Ellen, find out where August has been hiding."

The urge to get Laurel to talk about something else and wipe away that anxious expression, to learn more about her before she left them forever, took over. "Tell me about your foster family. The Heigels. What were they like?"

"Annaliese was a concert pianist. She played for the San

Francisco Symphony Orchestra for many years. Her husband, Gary, owned a car dealership. They were as different as two people could be." She smiled wistfully. "They lost their only child, a son, Gary Jr., to a drive-by shooting a few years before my dad died. My dad was put on the case and worked for months to track the suspect and round up eyewitnesses who weren't afraid to testify."

"Sounds like your dad was a bulldog."

"He *was* very focused, and very good at his job. I don't remember much with the Heigels' case, and they never really shared about it, but my dad mentioned them from time to time. He said they had been grateful for justice for their son and closure of the case."

"What a tragic loss." He glanced at her. "So how is it that they were available to take you in?"

"After the bust at the laundromat, my dad must've realized his life was in danger. I didn't know it at the time, but he contacted Gary. Met with them. They agreed to take care of me if something happened to him."

"No grandparents?"

"No. My parents had me later in life. My mom's parents were in a nursing home when I visited them as a little girl, and they both passed before I was five. My dad's mom was physically healthy but unfortunately had dementia and couldn't raise a child."

"God bless the Heigels for taking you in."

"Yes. They *were* a blessing, even when I was a stinker and refused to come down for dinner. Even when I cried for days about missing my dad."

"It sounds like they understood your pain, and gave you grace about your grieving process."

"They did. They had lost their only child, and I had lost my only parent. I think it bonded us." She sniffled. "They were so in love, even after all those years, and once Annaliese lost her battle to cancer, Gary wasn't far behind."

"I'm sorry you had to deal with losing them too."

"Thanks, Heath." Her sincere words dug under his skin.

Thirty minutes later they drove through the quaint town of Franklin. Cozy storefronts and lights strung across the main street, and Heath watched as boisterous families out for lunch and businesspeople in a hurry jostled along the sidewalk, entering restaurants and shopping for antiques.

"She lives near the woods, just north of the city. Only a couple neighbors nearby." Heath pulled off the main street and turned right. The truck ascended a hill, and the homes and businesses thinned out. A sliver of doubt twinged his skin like a splinter. Once they reached the top, he shot her a quick look.

"There will be two other officers there. Not sure who yet. Eli is in Corry processing the vehicle they found Angelo Costa in, but he's aware of the situation and will bring backup if needed."

Laurel nodded but remained quiet. Pensive. The doubt returned, like a bee sting this time. Should he have taken her back to Holloway first? Risked missing his opportunity to speak with Ellen Basile and possibly find out August's location? At the moment, and for reasons he didn't want to admit to himself, he preferred not to be separated from her.

"Thank you, Heath," she repeated.

He tilted his head. "For what?"

"For staying with me. For caring. For not hating me because of what almost happened to Piper. For…all of it."

"Laurel…" He lay his left arm over the wheel to steer then clasped her hand with the other. There went his resolve to distance himself from her. "I'd do it all over again."

"Will you tell me something?" she asked suddenly.

"Sure."

"When we ran into the sweet older fisherman on the island that morning, he mentioned something about him owing you his life. But when I asked you about it, you waved it off. What was he talking about?"

He removed his hand from her arm, then brushed his palm along the top of the steering wheel. Why was she asking about that? "For the first time in my ten-year career in law enforcement, I had to use deadly force. In Carl Danson's house." He shook his head as they pulled down a narrow country lane.

"How awful. Were you…cleared of any wrongdoing?"

"Yes, but that doesn't really ease the guilt. The man who'd broken in was a threat, undoubtedly, but that didn't negate the fact he had an estranged wife. Kids." He checked his GPS. "Taking another person's life…was awful. Some men are empowered by it. Like a notch on their belt. For me, it was easily the hardest thing I've dealt with in my professional life."

"What a burden that must be. But Carl and his wife are alive because of it," she noted.

"That's true."

A car approached from behind, and Heath's pulse kicked up. Laurel must've heard the engine, too, and she whipped around.

"It's local PD. We're good." He relaxed, and she expelled a huge breath.

Heath consulted the map again. "We're coming up on the driveway. I'm going to park out on the road with the other two officers. I'll stay here unless they need me. I'd like to be on hand to question Ellen myself, then we'll head back to Holloway."

Laurel nodded, but he didn't miss how pale her skin appeared.

As they neared the woman's rural residence, Heath surveyed their surroundings. Thick woods lined the pothole-infested road, and crooked mailboxes stuck up along the roadside, marking homes that were nearly invisible behind the trees.

"Her double-wide sits about two hundred yards back there."

The other car pulled around and came up beside them. A middle-aged, balding man rolled the window down. He wore a dark green uniform, and his clean-shaven face held a stern look of authority.

"Sergeant Calhoun?"

"Yes, sir. You must be Sergeant Gilbert. You have another officer on the way?"

"That is correct. Officer Waterford. ETA is one minute. Waterford and I will go in, ask to see the resident. If she's not home, we'll inspect the property and leave a note."

"You have the warrant?"

"Sure do. The judge sped up the warrant process based on your statements and the evidence from the airport authorities, and we have that in hand."

"Excellent." Heath lowered his voice. "Be on alert. Cop killer August Basile may be here."

"Understood. Let's start by seeing who's home. I'll apprise you of the situation and we'll go from there."

"Sounds good. Thanks."

"Here, take this." Sergeant Gilbert handed Heath a spare two-way radio.

Just then another officer pulled up. Gilbert introduced Heath to Adam Waterford, then he climbed into the second police car and the two men crept down the driveway. Laurel and Heath watched their progress, and Heath fidgeted with the radio then unbuckled his seat belt.

"Do you want to go with them?"

"I'd rather not leave you alone." He pulled his weapon from the glove compartment and slipped it into his waist holster.

Her hands were knotted on her lap, then she unwound them and snatched a loose lock of hair, twining it anxiously.

He noted her nervousness. “It’s for worst-case scenarios.”

One minute ticked by. Then two. Because of the woods, it was impossible to see the woman’s house or monitor what was happening. Through the branches, bits of gray siding were visible, but that was it. The radio crackled to life.

“We knocked, but no one answered,” one of the men said. “Heard voices, though. We’re going around back to check the property. There’s a shed that looks suspiciously like it might house marijuana—”

The sound of a man shouting and gunfire exploded over the radio, scalding his eardrums.

“Ten thirty-three!” the man shouted. “Backup!”

Laurel gasped as Heath pressed the gas. They shot down the driveway, toward the trailer and the mounting turmoil.

FIFTEEN

Laurel gripped the console as Heath's truck flew halfway down the driveway. He slammed it into Park thirty yards from a gray-and-blue double-wide trailer then shouted into his cell, requesting backup from a dispatcher. Weeds and overgrown trees encroached on much of the lane, covering their location. Through the trees, a flash of movement caught Laurel's eye as a thin, brown-haired female flung open the door, screaming and gesturing wildly.

"That's the woman from the airport," Laurel cried.

"Officer down!" crackled over the radio.

Laurel pressed her hands to her heart. *God, help them.*

"Recline your seat and stay down." Heath opened the door and unholstered his gun. "I'll take position in the woods in case I get a sighting of the suspect. See, right there? It's not far. Our other backup should be here soon."

"Be careful," she pleaded as he exited the vehicle and rushed into the woods directly in front of the trailer. She huddled low in the seat, sitting upright just enough to watch what was happening in the woods between the truck and the trailer.

"God, please keep him safe." For three days she'd pushed aside how much Heath affected her. How much he had come to mean to her. She was a fool to keep lying to herself.

While they would never have a future together, Heath Calhoun would be so easy to lean fully on, to tell all her secrets to. *To love.*

Suddenly Sergeant Gilbert sprinted around the house. A man clad in low-slung jeans and a black tank top followed him, waving a rifle. Laurel squinted. Could that be August? The man had shaggy blond hair and shouted obscenities as Sergeant Gilbert dashed for cover, the radio to his face. Heath held still behind a stand of oak trees, his body taut as the armed man slowed, swaggering after Sergeant Gilbert. Had he gotten Gilbert's gun away from him?

"Ten thirty-three! Ten thirty-three!" Gilbert's voice burst from the walkie-talkie in the truck, and she winced at the volume. Heath adjusted his position so he could follow the unfolding action.

When the man aimed the weapon at Gilbert, Heath shouted something, and Gilbert dived toward the squad car, hitting the driveway with a hard thud. A shower of gravel and dust bloomed above his head, and the crack of a gun sounded.

Who had been shot?

Laurel gaped at the scene unfolding before her eyes. Poor Heath. He had just admitted to her how much he despised having to shoot anyone.

"That was a warning." Heath's booming voice sounded. "Police. Drop the weapon or I will shoot."

The armed man sneered, shouting a colorful string of oaths at him. Laurel tried to focus on the man's face, to make out if that skinny, disheveled person could be August, but she couldn't take her eyes off Heath. He stood safely behind the trees, but one wrong move…

Her heart flip-flopped. She'd lost so many people in life. She couldn't lose him, too.

"God, please protect Heath and the other officers. Bring their backup soon."

The armed man aimed again, and Laurel sucked in a breath as Heath pulled away from the tree to aim as well. A pop sounded and the violent gunman dropped, his sneer morphing to shock as red bloomed on his chest. Laurel slapped her hand over her mouth as the woman on the front porch screamed and fell toward the downed man.

Sergeant Gilbert rose from his spot behind his car and motioned at Heath. The two men shouted back and forth, then Gilbert jogged over to the wounded suspect, warning the woman back.

Heath glanced back at her, and even from thirty or forty yards away, she noted the distress on his handsome face.

Suddenly his features changed, and he gestured wildly at her.

Motion in her left peripheral vision snagged her attention from Heath just as the glass shattered on the truck's driver-side window. Laurel screamed as a man wearing a dark beanie pulled low over his forehead yanked the door open and shoved himself into the vehicle, stabbing the ignition, then reaching one wiry arm across to grab her wrists and shackle them together.

"I got you now." When he looked at her, everything stilled. An ugly, puckered scar ran the length of his face on the left side, from brow to chin. A scream rose in her throat as he shifted into Reverse and flew backward up the driveway.

August Basile had found her.

Heath didn't have time to think. He just acted. August had started up his truck and peeled out, crashing into bushes and decapitating a small tree in the process.

He erupted from the bushes and raced after his truck, but they were on the road now and he stood no chance of catching up. He veered back toward the second squad car and shouted at Sergeant Gilbert.

"Keys! I need your car," he yelled at Gilbert. The other sergeant grabbed a set of handcuffs and the tactical medical kit from the back and tossed his key at Heath.

Gilbert rushed back to the woman, who leaned over the wounded man, wailing. Now, Heath's focus was on Laurel. He did a U-turn, then gunned the squad car in pursuit of his truck. This was the opposite way they'd driven in here, and if he remembered correctly from studying the map on the plane, the road dead-ended a couple of miles from her trailer and connected to several trails that led to a park set on a lake.

"God, please help me find her in time." Every moment of the last three days ran through his mind, from the first time he saw Laurel at the swamp to the last time he bade her goodbye, just moments ago. He didn't know her well—yet—but he was certain there was something between them. A spark he'd never felt with anyone other than his wife.

Kara. Heath's throat closed as he sped toward the dead end. *I will always love you, baby. You are Piper's mom and my first big love. But I might be able to fall in love with Laurel, and I wish I could get your permission.*

He ground his jaw and swiped at his cheek, then spotted the truck parked awkwardly near a trailhead at the dead end. August moved fast, but he'd move faster. Heath roared up to the truck in the squad car and slammed the brakes. Gravel flew. He jumped out, clutching his weapon as the faraway wail of sirens carried down the road.

Backup.

No time to wait. He jogged past his truck, following the footsteps to a trail on the north side of the dead end. Heath's stride hitched as he ran, keeping his upper body hunched low and his senses alert.

A woman's cry shattered the quiet, and a flock of birds burst from the trees. There. About fifty yards ahead. Instead of tracking them directly, Heath cut to the right and pushed through the brush, keeping his steps light. He had one chance, one opportunity to surprise August.

Lord willing, Laurel was still okay.

He needed her. He'd only just met her, but he already knew, just as he'd known with Kara, that having Laurel in his life would be almost as important as oxygen. He couldn't let something happen to her before he told her how he felt.

"Stop it." A man's snarling voice slithered through the woods, and he edged toward it. What was August's endgame with her? The lake? Did he not care he was about to be cornered by a dozen law enforcement officers?

Heath's blood pressure spiked. He couldn't let that criminal get Laurel any closer to the water. Up ahead, a small structure—a dilapidated boathouse—caught his eye.

Movement grabbed his attention. August dragged Laurel toward the boathouse. Her hands were clasped together by something—rope maybe—as she stumbled along, crying.

You're not alone. I'm coming.

He sidestepped a rotted stump and almost tripped over the massive roots that remained. So much like the terrible situation unfolding right now. August Basile's bitterness had taken root and controlled his life. Heath ground his back teeth. That would end now. Today.

Heath inched closer to the boathouse. It appeared that the structure was three-sided, not four. The front was doorless, directly overlooking the water.

Dread scurried down his spine like a rat on a pipe. If August knew Heath was coming after him, he would expect him to appear in the open side facing the lake. He had to take a different approach.

Heath checked once more for August, then scuttled toward the boathouse. As he approached the back side, he sank to all fours and crawled through the grass and dirt. The structure was built up on cinder block, maybe three feet off the earth. Enough room to sidle beneath.

He holstered his weapon then crawled military style through an opening between the cinder blocks. A spiderweb spread across his face, and he swiped it off. Shadows shrouded the ground beneath the boathouse, but Heath could still make out rocks, a slimy old oar, and the spiny feel of fish bones here and there. The stench of rotted meat wafted about, and his stomach revolted. When he tilted his head to look at the underside of the floor, his jaw unhinged. The floor slats were worn, and in some sections daylight sliced through the wood panels. Heath prayed he wasn't visible from above. He eyed the boards, carefully testing their strength. As he neared the front of the boathouse, he noticed the boards' color changed from solid brown to a mold-caked, spongy green.

Voices carried down to him as he inspected the structure's base for weaknesses.

"I wasn't even going to bother with this, but you and that police officer from Holloway gave my guys so much trouble, now I have to." August snarled. "It's better this way. More satisfying."

"Leave him out of this."

"I don't care about him and his kid. You're the one who's going to pay. Your stupid cop dad murdered my father, and messed up my family. Then you ruined my life when you did this. Do you see this?" He cursed. "You made me look like a monster!"

"I was a child, defending myself."

He let out a sarcastic snort. "You should've killed me when

you had the chance, Lauralee Campbell." August's footsteps creaked across the floor, just above Heath's head.

Please, God. Show me when, Heath prayed as he crawled carefully toward the fourth, open wall. He ran his fingertips along the wood slats as he moved. Soft spots met his skin in several places. Water and time had rotted out many of the floorboards, just as time and bitterness had rotted away August's soul.

This would be the best angle to shoot from below.

He scooted back to where she sat tied to the chair, his cheeks puffed up with exertion. August leaned over her, shouting.

"Look at me! Look what you did to me."

"I would never have shot you if you hadn't come after my dad and killed him." Laurel's tear-threaded voice pinched Heath's heart. She sounded terrified, and it took all his self-control not to bust through the front of the boathouse and open fire. Too risky. Laurel might be shot or wounded in the fray.

He'd just found her, and he couldn't lose her now.

Heath angled his head just right, then he could see a portion of her hair and face through the slits in the floor. Just barely.

God, help me please. Help me figure out how to get her out of here safely.

"Your cop dad stole it all away from me. Everything. That money was supposed to be mine."

"It would never have been yours. Your dad was going to have your brother lead your crime ring family, not you."

"You're lying!" Something shot out, and Laurel screeched, then a hard *thump* followed. She whimpered, and Heath flinched. His free hand curled into a fist. August had kicked at the chair she was tied to, and it had fallen to the side, Laurel with it.

"Before I throw you in the lake, I want you to feel how I felt. I want your pretty little face to look like mine." A long silver blade glinted in the sunlight, and Laurel's whimpers turned to desperate wails.

Wisps of her dark hair peeked through the flooring, and his fingers twitched. He needed to let her know he was there, and to try and get August closer to the boathouse opening. If he whispered too softly, Laurel wouldn't hear him. If he whispered too loud, they both might be dead.

Heath jimmied his large frame up to where her chair lay sideways, squinting and searching for her face. There. Only an inch or two separated them, and Heath's gut clenched at how much he cared for this woman. How much he needed her to be okay. To be with him.

He pressed his mouth to the wood. "Laurel."

Nothing.

He spoke again. "Laurel. I'm here."

She jolted, lifting her head then angling her face so he could see one of her eyes and the edge of her poor wounded mouth.

"Your ankles aren't tied. Kick him, get him closer to the opening."

She lay her head back on the floor and huffed in heavy breaths, moaning and crying. What—

She was using her tears as a cover. Heath positioned himself on his back, pushed closer to the boathouse's open wall, and adjusted his arms and aim. The gun sights lined up with the soggiest, most rotted-out boards.

"What are you crying about now?" August righted her chair with a frustrated grunt. "Sit up and shut it. Where should we get you all prettied up before I throw you in the lake? Your cheek—here—or your lips. Aw, looks like you already got a hit to your perfect mouth. Or—hey!"

A blur of motion exploded above him, and August bellowed as he stumbled backward.

"Now!" Laurel cried.

Heath lined up his sights at a specific angle through the green wood and pulled the trigger.

The noise blasted into his eardrums, but Heath held steady and aimed again. There was a low groan, then a thud. Laurel sobbed, and Heath shot out between the cinder blocks and leapt up into the boathouse. August lay on his side, blood streaming from the gunshot wound in his thigh.

But then he rolled to his stomach with an inhuman howl and pushed upright. He wobbled before Heath, defiant, then edged backward, toward Laurel, the knife glinting in his shaking grasp.

"You think…you can keep her safe. She will never…be safe again."

Heath aimed the gun, his mouth dry and his heartbeat steady. Laurel's eyes widened as August pivoted and dived at her, the knife held out.

He fired, hitting dead center mass before August's body rotated all the way. August flopped to the ground, completely still as more blood bloomed from a gunshot wound to his chest.

Heath rushed over, weapon trained and used his shoe to nudge August. He felt for a pulse. Nothing. He stepped over the criminal and fell to his knees in front of Laurel, scrambling to untie her bonds. Then he pulled her from the chair and lifted her to him, his arms wrapping her tightly. "I'm here. Hey, you're safe."

She clutched him. "You came."

"I told you that you wouldn't be alone again."

"Is he…?"

"Dead?" Heath expelled a breath that it felt like he'd been

holding since August nabbed Laurel. "Yes." He craned his neck as men shouted nearby. "In here. Suspect is down." He set her back on her feet and looked her over, tracing his fingers under her chin to inspect the cut over her lip. "They'll need to make sure you're not hurt. Are you?"

She shook her head, her beautiful eyes pinned to him. "Don't leave me, please." She clasped one of his hands.

He held it and kept her close as officers entered the boathouse and marked the scene. Heath called out what happened, keeping the details short, then he and Laurel climbed down the stairs and stood beside the structure.

"I couldn't believe it when I heard your voice below the floor." She sagged into him. "I knew I wasn't alone. God was with me. He was my strength, just like the verse said. I was weak, but He was strong. Then *you* came."

He pivoted so he stood in front of her, then cupped one of her cheeks, stroking away dirt-streaked tears. "If I had my way, you'd never be alone again." Had he said that aloud?

Her eyes widened at his words. "Do you mean…?"

"I…" He just knew that he needed her. That he didn't want to let her go.

"Wait, Heath Calhoun is at a loss for words?"

His mouth quirked. "There are words I'd like to say, and there are things I'd like to do, but I don't know if you'd let me, especially with this." He gestured at the small cut on her lip.

She stood on her tippy toes, drawing them closer. "Try me."

He blinked, and the sunlight dousing the aged boathouse highlighted Laurel's smooth skin and damp, luminous brown eyes. She wasn't Kara, and that was okay. She was an entirely different, incredible, unique person, and Heath was filled with the warm realization that his wife would've loved Laurel. Would've approved of her and Heath together.

"If you insist." Heath cradled Laurel's face and gently kissed her. Her soft lips and the affection in her eyes before they closed sent a whirlwind of emotion through him.

Relief. Gratitude. Joy.

He pulled back and swept her up into his arms again, and only when the other officers swarmed the area did he pull away. Just then an EMT arrived and addressed Heath.

"Anyone wounded?"

"The suspect is deceased. She needs to be checked out." Heath motioned at Laurel.

Fifteen minutes later Heath had given his statement, surrendered his gun for now and watched as August Basile's lifeless body was strapped on a gurney and taken to the local morgue. While he had never wanted to take another person's life again, the situation had called for it and he had no regrets.

Laurel finished with the paramedics, then joined him near his truck, her stride sluggish but her smile bright. Undimmed by fear. Finally.

When she reached him, Heath tugged her close, running his hands down her arms then cupping her elbows to draw her even closer. "I've been thinking..."

"About the kiss?" She grinned. "Me, too."

"Yeah, about that." He captured a long lock of hair framing her face, twining it around his finger like he'd seen her do. "But I don't want to hurt your mouth."

"We'll take it easy. For now." She grinned.

He grinned back, a sense of wonder washing over him, cleaning away the guilt and regret. What an unexpected gift God had given him with this woman. With Laurel. "I think I could really... There could be a lot there with us..."

She stood on her tippy toes. "I know. Me, too."

Then Heath kissed her again, the warmth of the sun shining down on their new beginning as tomorrow stretched out before them.

EPILOGUE

Laurel slowed as she approached the ranger station. Her feet hurt and her muscles ached, but it had been worth it. She'd spent nearly all day in the forest, cataloging the changing leaves on four different trees for the US Forest Service's latest website updates. The Commonwealth of Pennsylvania administrator had contacted her last month, at the end of September, to see if she was available to capture fall in all its glory in northwestern Pennsylvania.

Of course, she'd said yes. What an honor for her work to be used on the state's website. After taking two hundred shots today, she was confident she'd captured the beauty of this area as fall arrived and said goodbye to summer.

She tilted her head as something colorful crossed the ranger station window on the inside of the building. What was that? Maybe Tucker had his red jacket on again. The temps *had* dropped lately. She checked her phone, a flash of disappointment hollowing out her chest. Today was her birthday, and while Heath had texted her a sweet message that morning, she hadn't heard from him since.

The months since August Basile's men had come after her at the swamp had passed quickly. Once August's body was identified, the estate of Leonard Basile paid for him to be flown to California to be buried beside his notorious family members. The man Heath had shot at Ellen Basile's trailer was another parolee who had helped in the plot to come after Laurel. Only Ellen Basile remained alive from the infamous crime family, and she was spending the next five years behind bars for aggravated assault, threatening the life of a police officer and illegal possession of marijuana.

Director Alex Vegas had notified them that two men were apprehended by authorities after robbing a bank near the Bay then taking off in the same SUV that had tailed her and Heath across the Golden Gate Bridge. Both men had served time while August was in prison, and they were arrested. Alex had taken Laurel's case to the Attorney General and asked that she be allowed to stay in Holloway now that all the suspects were in custody.

Or dead.

Laurel shivered, shaking off the emotions of that awful day when Heath had confronted August at the boathouse. He was gone. Forever. *Thank You, Lord.*

Heath had helped her find an apartment in his sister Katie's complex, and she had been welcomed into the Calhoun and Buchanan families. Summer barbecues, family board games and Friday evening talks by the fire pit while roasting marshmallows at Heath's with him and Piper had given her a joy and contentment she'd never experienced before.

Thank You, Lord.

She smiled, pushing away the disappointment that she might not see Heath and Piper until later, when they had planned to meet for dinner in town with his dad and sisters and Eli. She had so much to thank God for, sometimes it overwhelmed her.

She grabbed the ranger station door handle and opened it, then shrieked and jumped back when a dozen people tumbled toward her instead of just Tucker. Bright balloons danced around the large, cleared-out room, streamers flew through the air, and people shouted, "Surprise!"

Laurel grinned, tears prickling her eyes as Piper and Skylar dashed over.

"Happy, happy birthday, Ms. Laurel!" Piper threw herself into Laurel's arms, and she hoisted the lightweight child in one of those quick, tight hugs she'd come to love. "Guess what my daddy is—"

"Shhh," Skylar warned, sending a big-eyed look at Piper, then the two little girls fell into a conversation of gestures, smiles and head shakes much like the silent conversation Heath and Molly had that day at the swamp.

What were they up to? She hugged them both back then turned to the adults.

"I can't believe this!" Laurel exclaimed, trying to take it in. Her face already ached from smiling so big, and she ventured deeper into the unrecognizable station, taking turns hugging those who had become so dear to her. First Molly—who glowed with a sweet little secret only a few people knew—then Eli, Katie and the rest of the Calhoun and Buchanan families. Sarah Brindley, Tucker's beautiful fiancée, ran over and offered a hug, her adorable son Liam peeking out from behind her.

Where was—

"Laurel." Heath's deep voice pulled at her. She turned, and he stood in the doorway, filling it—and her heart—a look of adoration on his handsome face. Was he truly hers?

"I'll be right back." She grinned at Sarah and Molly, who sent her a pair of saucy smiles in return.

What was that about? She was still learning the humorous Calhoun family language of waggling brows and lopsided smiles.

"Where were you hiding?" Laurel stepped outside the door and set her hands to her hips playfully.

He pointed to the canoe rack out back, where Tucker had erected a shed and cover over the ranger canoes. Then he clasped her hand and pulled her farther out, to a patch of grass bathed in soft yellow light from the evening sun.

In view of the ranger station and their families and friends.

"Did you plan all this?" She stepped closer, overcome by her deep love for this thoughtful, outspoken man.

"Part of it. Molly, Katie, and Sarah planned the rest."

"Thank you all. This means so much, though I'm kind of embarrassed at all the attention."

"Don't be. This is your special day." He reached for her hands, drawing her flush against him in a quick, tight embrace much like his daughter's, yet very different. He pecked her hair, then stepped back. "Happy birthday, my beautiful Laurel. Were you surprised?"

"Very. I still am. I love it. What part did you plan?"

"This one." Suddenly Heath knelt before her, holding out a small blue box in his large palm. Laurel's heart somersaulted, and she covered her mouth. A woman in the ranger station whooped. Was he—

"Heath?"

Another person whooped—that was definitely Molly—and Heath sent a stern but playful look toward the open door, where a dozen beloved faces peeked out. The girls were near the bottom, their scrunched-up, excited expressions making Laurel laugh and cry at the same time.

"Laurel Grace Bell, I never expected anyone like you in my life. You're kind and funny, smart and giving. You love me and Piper so well…something I wasn't sure we would ever have again." He swiped at his eye, then motioned Piper outside, and tears stung Laurel's throat. "We want you to be part of our family. Forever. Don't we, Piper?"

"Ms. Laurel, I miss Mommy. But I know she's with Jesus.

I think He sent you so I can have another mommy. Daddy really wants to marry you, and I want him to, too. Forge really, *really* likes you. And you rub my back really good and you make the best chocolate chip muffins. Okay it's your turn again, Daddy." Piper hopped back, grinning.

He stood and stepped closer, slowly slipping the beautiful solitaire on her finger. "Will you marry me—marry us?"

Laurel barely held back tears that felt very much like a baptism into a new life. A life filled with family and grace, and lots of love.

She drew Piper in between them and threw her arms around Heath's broad shoulders, shoulders that helped her carry the weight of her past. "Yes, I want to marry you, Heath, and I would love to join your family, Piper. I love you both so much."

Heath cradled her face, and they joined their watery, gleeful grins together. Then he kissed her, but not before meeting Laurel's eyes and promising a lifetime of togetherness.

* * * * *

Dear Reader,

Thank you for reading Targeted in the Swamp. I've grown quite close to the characters in my Forest Ranger Rescuers series, and I'm thrilled Heath Calhoun now has his own happily-ever-after. I knew I needed a special person for him, and I came to love Laurel and her longing for a home and family to call her own.

One of the most amazing gifts that comes with trusting in Jesus is knowing that through His sacrifice on the cross, believers become part of the family of God—sisters and brothers in Christ. For those who haven't experienced a forever family, I pray God reminds you that you are His child, He loves you and He will never leave you or forsake you.

I love staying in touch with readers! Look for me on Facebook (Kerry Johnson Author), Instagram or on my website, www.kerryjohnsonbooks.com, where you can sign up for my quarterly newsletter. God bless you and keep you.

Fondly,
Kerry Johnson